MURDER
AT THE ROYAL
SHAKESPEARE

Teresa Collard

This first world edition published in Great Britain 1994 by
SEVERN HOUSE PUBLISHERS LTD of
9–15 High Street, Sutton, Surrey SM1 1DF.
First published in the USA 1994 by
SEVERN HOUSE PUBLISHERS INC., of
425 Park Avenue, New York, NY 10022.

British Library Cataloguing in Publication Data
Collard, Teresa
  Murder at the Royal Shakespeare
  I. Title
  823.914 [F]

  ISBN 0-7278-4581-0
        0-7278-9014-X (trade paperback)

Typeset by Hewer Text Composition Services, Edinburgh.
Printed and bound in Great Britain by
Redwood Books, Trowbridge, Wiltshire.

For Catherine, Ed, Beth and Daniel Baines

Acknowledgements

I am especially indebted to Graham Sawyer who
led me through the labyrinthine ways of The Royal
Shakespeare Theatre, and to the late Hugh Ross
Williamson for inspiration gained from his book *The
Day Shakespeare Died*.

Thanks also to Philip Ash, John Fennell, Joe McGloin,
Denise and Ed Hunt and Tony Wootton.

Prologue

It was a strange feeling; like coming home. A school outing, twenty-five years ago, to Stratford-upon-Avon to see *Julius Caesar* had changed his life.

Old Hedley, his form master, with a string of twenty boys in his care, had made up his mind that not one would fall at the first hurdle. Never mind what else they did or didn't do, he would make sure they passed O level English literature.

The boys, armed with sandwiches, cans of coke, notebooks and pencils, had been bussed to Stratford in a rickety old coach. As well as attending a performance of *Julius Caesar* they'd been given a project, and woe betide any of the young scholars who didn't see it through. Two weeks in which to come up with a 1500 word essay on Shakespeare's life and background.

In the morning Hedley walked the boys round the town. They saw where Shakespeare had been born, where he'd gone to school and, New Place, the site on which the large house he'd acquired in his affluent later life had stood. They saw everything except Anne Hathaway's cottage at Shottery. First of all, the party led by the aging schoolmaster, had visited Holy Trinity, the Parish Church, to see the actual spot in the chancel where the Bard was buried. After that they were shown a facsimile of the Register in which the baptism on 26th April, 1564 of William, son of John and Mary Shakespeare, was recorded.

Hedley, with great pride, drew their attention to a bust on the north wall of the choir. James Byrd remembered the old man lifting his arm as he pointed to the poet's brow, as though he had been the sculptor.

'There in that head,' he had said, 'were kindled the ideas for the world's greatest plays by the world's greatest playwright.'

7

The noble brow didn't capture the interest of his young charges. Most of the lads were more interested in the misericords on the choir stalls for they giggled uncontrollably at the naked body of a woman astride a stag, and a chained ape providing a specimen of its urine in a small flask. Old Hedley was annoyed that such gross fantasies were of more interest than the alabaster bust.

Byrd remembered thinking that Shakespeare, as a young lad, would have seen the misericords, and probably giggled in the same way. 400 years didn't change human nature.

The bust, Hedley had said, was reputedly the most accurate likeness of the great man despite the fact that it made him look more like a divine than an actor.

Young James Byrd had tackled old Hedley's project with enthusiasm. He'd even cycled from Oxford to Snitterfield, a small village near Stratford, where William's grandfather Richard Shakespeare had farmed from 1529 until his death. There he made strenuous efforts to trace other antecedents. He wrote a fulsome essay, nearer 3000 words than 1500, on the lad whose father, a prosperous glover of good yeoman stock, had married into the gentry and who eventually became High Bailiff of the borough.

In his research he discovered that Shakespeare, at the age of 18, married Anne Hathaway 8 years older than himself, who was carrying his child. They married in November 1582, and Susanna was born the following May.

He was quite thrilled to discover that in 1584, William, who may well have been a wild tempestuous youth, had been poaching on the estates of Sir Thomas Lucy, and as a consequence hurriedly left for London. Old Hedley had been furious.

'His peccadilloes, which may well be mythical, have little to do with his development as a great playwright. Much more to the point if you'd recorded the hours he spent at the Grammar School. From 5.45 in the mornings, home for lunch and then back again until 6.45 in the evening. And why, for heaven's sake, do you keep harking back to his grandfather?'

'I want to trace his ancestry, sir.'

'That problem, Byrd, has floored an army of academics, and wasting time on such matters won't get you through your exam.'

It was at that moment young James Byrd made the most important decision in his life. He liked delving, talking to villagers, asking questions, reading old documents, searching for the truth, cycling round the countryside, but he didn't fancy being tucked away in a musty library in academia . . . no none of that!

Young James Byrd knew exactly what his role in life would be.

Chapter 1

Foul deeds will rise,
Though all the earth o'erwhelm them, to men's eyes.
For murder, though it have no tongue, will speak
With most miraculous organ.

'Low key.' said Sir Charles Suckling emphatically. 'I've had a word with my opposite number in Warwickshire who says he has no spare personnel to deal with fantasies. Thinks it pie in the sky, but is not averse to us dabbling, so give it two days, Mr Byrd, in that temple of Thespis. Detective Superintendent James Byrd mused on those words as he drove from his cottage in Bletchingdon to the Royal Shakespeare Theatre in Stratford-upon-Avon wondering whether it was tempting fate to mention Thespis, the founder of Greek tragedy,

Keaton, his immediate boss and nicknamed Buster, would have scorned such thoughts. It was a straight-forward enquiry which didn't need the services of a superintendent, nevertheless he was pleased to see the back of Byrd on yet another secondment, no matter how short.

Byrd, who was early, parked his car in the space reserved for him and walked alongside the Avon to take a better look at Clopton Bridge. A fifteenth-century miracle given to the town by Sir Hugh Clopton a local benefactor who became Lord Mayor of London. Its fourteen arches, supporting an ever increasing avalanche of traffic, had stood the test of time. A bridge Shakespeare would have crossed on his way to London. He stood gazing at the swans and pleasure boats plying their trade up and down the river. He'd not thought of May as a busy month, but the town was full of Japanese, Germans and Americans

10

on culture tours, and gaggles of schoolchildren who would later attend a matinée in a last desperate attempt to learn a little more before their June exams.

At precisely five minutes to eleven he presented himself at the box office and within seconds was whisked through a pass door and found himself shaking hands with Vivian Mollington, the Artistic Director, a man tall as himself, bearded too, greying prematurely, and wearing a multi-coloured shirt with tassels round the bottom. A fashion that even the way-out policeman considered bizarre. A charming extrovert, thought Byrd, with steel in his make-up.

Mollington introduced him to John Butler, the General Manager, more conservatively dressed in a light grey suit and pale blue shirt which matched his pale blue eyes.

Butler, a small quiet man, in whose office they were meeting smiled at the visitor. The smile from this phlegmatic character, an accountant and administrator, who controlled the fortunes of the world's most famous theatre from an office hardly much bigger than a broom cupboard, said it all. A warning that he, like the Chief Constable of Warwickshire, thought this exercise totally unnecessary.

Gerald Maitland, Manager and Licensee, the youngest man in the room, who was dressed in a denim shirt and jeans, towered above them all. He shook hands, winked at Butler, an action not missed by the policeman, and sat down.

'We'd better get down to the nitty gritty,' said Mollington as he poured a cup of coffee for his guest. 'I'm in the throes of the final rehearsals for *The Tempest*, and can't afford to miss this afternoon's run-through. My assistant director had a couple of wisdom teeth extracted this morning, most inconvenient, so the stage manager's coping, but she'll need time this afternoon to check properties and liaise with wardrobe.'

He spread his left hand on the table examined his nails before clenching and unclenching his fist. His fevered imaginings sounded wilder every time he repeated them. Perhaps he'd gone too far involving his uncle, a busy Chief Constable, in all this? But it was too late now, the policeman who'd been given two days to delve into the matter sat there, looking at him. Waiting.

'How much do you know, Mr Byrd?'

The shirt was too much for Byrd, it dazzled him, but he was amused when he met Mollington's gaze to find his eyes were also multicoloured. One grey . . . one hazel.

'I only know what Sir Charles has told me, but I'd rather have it from the horse's mouth.'

'OK I'll spell it out.' He waved his hands in a magnificent histrionic gesture. 'John and Gerald both think it's all in my mind, a scenario for an Agatha Christie, but I blame myself for not noticing the signs earlier. Had I done so I'm sure Sally Siddons wouldn't have gone missing.'

'What signs, Mr Mollington? Hadn't you better start at the beginning?'

'Yes, of course. Sally, as you may remember from the newspaper reports last year, vanished five days after *Romeo and Juliet* opened. The critics were lavish in their praise. Another Ashcroft. Another Dench. One of the Nationals, may have been the *Daily Mirror*, went too far . . . said acting was in her genes . . . her ancestry shone through.'

'You mean Siddons?'

'Yes. *The Tragic Muse*, none other. They were hopelessly off beam, but we didn't correct the assumption. She chose Siddons, a good choice, because Equity wouldn't accept her as a member unless she changed her surname. There's already one Sally Brown in the profession. A name like Siddons is more likely to be noted by a theatre-going public.' Mollington sighed as he fiddled with the tassels on his shirt tail. 'She was attractive, had a good figure and would eventually have played all the Shakespearean heroines as Dench has done. The world, Superintendent, was hers for the asking. She had everything going for her, but what neither I nor the cast could understand was the change in her personality during the six weeks rehearsal period. Nerves, I thought. She was presented with the part of a lifetime, and yet somehow she couldn't take the weight, nor the responsibility, neither could she communicate with her fellow actors.

Before rehearsals began she'd been happy-go-lucky, a great socialiser, always joining in 'Donkey' with gusto, and wonderful as Nerissa in *The Merchant* the previous season.'

'Donkey!'

Mollington laughed. 'It's a damned silly game we play, usually with twelve participants. We begin with eleven spoons, always one fewer than the number of players. One of the stage management usually volunteers to manipulate the tape recorder. The spoons are passed round the table until the music stops, and the person who's left without a spoon stands on a chair and recites part of a quotation. The declaimer then points to one of the actors still sitting who has to complete the quote. If the actor fails then he or she is out of the game. If the quotation is completed then the player standing is out and has to remove a chair and a spoon, and so on until one player is left. It can be a hilarious game, a game Sally loved but halfway through rehearsals she gave up. In fact she gave up the day after ejecting Nigel from her lodging.'

'Who's Nigel?'

'Nigel Fisher, our answer to Errol Flynn. I'm sure you can't have missed those flashing eyes and cavalier manner he's adopted for his latest TV role. He's made quite a name for himself, but fortunately for us he prefers treading the boards. For a time he and Sally lived together in their own dream world, their own Utopia. We all thought it a perfect arrangement. Both up and coming young actors with similar interests, but soon after rehearsals for *Romeo* began, in which Nigel played Mercutio, he found himself unceremoniously ejected from Sally's lodging, and all his worldly goods dumped on the doorstep.'

'Where were they living?'

'33, Waterside, opposite the theatre,' said Gerald Maitland suppressing a yawn. 'Sally rented one of the small terraced houses which belong to the Royal Shakespeare Company. We have a great deal of property in Stratford which we let out to actors. Digs, as you can imagine, are hard to find. Sally was there for nearly two years.'

James Byrd finished his cold coffee. The disappearance

13

of an actress who had everything going for her made even less sense now he knew she'd been a happy-go-lucky soul living in a comfortable home with a lover who adored her. He'd seen Nigel Fisher in one of those ghastly soaps to which Kate was addicted. A tall, dark haired young man, a charming villain in *Pillow Talk*, an ongoing TV saga, who'd become his young daughter's pin-up.

'Have you any theories, Mr Mollington, about what might have happened?'

'A dozen theories, sir, but you'll want to hear about the most likely one.'

Byrd nodded.

'I thought, maybe, she was pregnant which could easily account for the personality change. She certainly lost her appetite, although from all accounts she never suffered from morning sickness, but having a child, maybe unwanted, could easily have changed her attitude towards Nigel.'

Not if she was truly in love with him, thought Byrd.

'She became withdrawn, lost weight, which nullified the pregnancy theory, and mooned about the place as if she'd just lost her nearest and dearest. Her performance at the penultimate rehearsal caused me a lot of soul searching. The question was whether to allow her to continue or bring in her understudy. The problem solved itself because her understudy caught flu. I was dreading the first night, I think we all were, but Sally went on and gave a truly great performance, captivating the audience. She was vivacious, loving, moving, and tragic, a true Juliet. Then five days later she vanished.'

'Did you contact the police?'

'They weren't interested. Sally left a note in her dressing room saying she didn't want to be found and, before you ask, it was in her handwriting.'

'There are hundreds of missing persons, so the police told me, and it's not in their remit to interfere.'

James Byrd glanced at John Butler who'd remained impassive throughout the saga.

'You don't see this as a matter for the police, Mr Butler?'

'No I don't, but my view is that of an outsider. Perhaps I would have been more aware of these changes if I'd been rehearsing eight hours a day for six weeks.'

'Do you still have the note she left?'

'Yes.'

Viv Mollington handed him a buff envelope, addressed quite simply, 'To Vivian'. The calligraphy struck Byrd as childlike but the first part of the missive was clear.

I go now of mine own accord. Look not for me.

But what did she mean by the second part?

Alack, alack! that heaven should practise stratagems
Upon so soft a subject as myself!

'Are you wondering, Mr Byrd which play these lines come from?'

'I read *Romeo* and *Macbeth* for A level so I recognise . . .'

'The Scottish play,' interrupted Viv, 'Never breathe the title except on the boards . . . it's bad luck.'

'For you, maybe, but not for me,' said the policeman annoyed at the interruption. 'I recognise the last two lines. They're from *Romeo and Juliet*, but the first one defeats me.'

'It has similarities to so many quotations but we think she made it up, and is telling us to leave well alone. Her parents came to the same conclusion.'

'But,' said Byrd, 'you can't leave well alone, and now, according to Sir Charles, similar circumstances with another young actress are causing anxiety.'

'Not anxiety, Mr Byrd. Fear. Fear knowing how one actor in a leading role can affect the rest of the cast.'

'You're going too far, Viv,' said Butler quietly. 'His trouble, Mr Byrd, is overwork. A meeting this morning, a rehearsal this afternoon, an appointment at the Barbican this evening which is, as I'm sure you know, our London base, and all that after a punishing drive down the M40. Viv, is doing the impossible.'

'Nothing you can say, John, will alter the fact that once again we're into the final rehearsals, and the change in Janet Shaw's personality is affecting us all. It's a repeat performance, I can't believe it's happening again.'

Bryd heard the despair. 'Which part is she playing?'

'Miranda. John thinks I'm making mountains out of molehills but a director lives through the characters on stage, he has to . . . has to understand the emotions and driving force. He also needs tremendous rapport with his actors. They are vulnerable people who need support, most of them totally different from their public image . . . they need to be nurtured, loved, coaxed, on occasions bullied, and constantly reassured. Their souls, don't you see, Mr Byrd, are bared. At the moment I can't get through to Janet, neither to her mind nor heart. She's shut me out.'

The quizzical smile on the General Manager's face riled Vivian Mollington.

'There's something evil happening in the theatre,' he growled, 'and if you'd sat through rehearsals you'd have felt the atmosphere.'

'Cool it, Viv,' said Gerald Maitland, 'We agree with you about Sally. The circumstances were odd, but you must admit your imagination works overtime. Why don't you persuade Janet to see a doctor?'

'I've tried. She doesn't want to know.' He turned to the policeman. 'I'm praying you can help us, Mr Byrd.'

'Not so fast, Mr Mollington. Let's get back to Sally Siddons, now missing for nearly a year. What about her parents, her close family and her friends? Surely they haven't let the matter drop?'

'Her parents weren't worried. Didn't want to discuss the matter. It was her brother who told me she'd done this sort of thing before, but wouldn't explain when or where. Mr Byrd, don't you see, I feel guilty about Sally, but I can do something about Janet.'

A bit late, thought the policeman, *waiting until the last week*.

'I'll do what I can, but I'll need a *raison dê'tre* to go everywhere, and see everything, especially rehearsals.'

16

'That means introducing you to the cast. I'll see how they feel about it.'

'What does that mean?'

'Rehearsals are sacrosanct . . . funny word to use . . . but it's true. Actors need to develop their roles . . . their relationships, their emotions, their reactions to a situation without an audience.'

'And one person presents an audience,' said the policeman acidly.

'Yes. Some come to grips with the part through their mind, others through their heart, but whatever the method, one person is an audience for which they're not ready.'

'If you want me to get on with the job, it's those reactions and relationships which may be pointers. I must see everything.'

'All right,' said Viv as if those two words had been dragged up from his boots. 'I'll talk with them. Incidentally, Mr Byrd, John has some ideas you should consider, really quite intelligent for an unimaginative man!'

The General Manager, who for the past hour had weighed up several possibilities, liked the bearded policeman, liked the informal dress, the denim suit, the purple shirt. He'd fit into the scheme he had in mind.

'I suggest, Mr Byrd, that you adopt the mantle of a management consultant. The whole world knows we're trying to cut costs. The role of consultant would enable you to be seen in every department of the theatre, even rehearsals as they're germane to your investigation, and of course see any performances you wish.'

'That sounds OK to me. When does *The Tempest* open?'

'In ten days time.'

'Then you'd better provide me with a clipboard and paper I'll get down to the job immediately.'

'Where do they rehearse?'

'In the Ashcroft Room above the Swan Theatre, which was built in 1986 and is Jacobean in style. It abuts the Victorian picture gallery and the main house. *Sophonisba* is rehearsing in The Swan, and *The Yorkshire Tragedy* at

The Other Place, that's the RSC's studio theatre down the road which we call the TOP.'

'Where do you want to begin?' asked Gerald.

'Better see a rehearsal or two for starters. Take a look at the protagonist in the case.'

Vivian glanced at his watch. 'They'll be breaking for lunch in about five minutes, an ideal moment to introduce you, then you can enjoy a snack lunch with me at the Dirty Duck, our local, which is opposite the Theatre Gardens and less than a hundred yards from the TOP.'

'Enjoy is not the word I'd use,' laughed John Butler. 'You forget, Mr Byrd will be working.'

Vivian ushered Byrd into the Ashcroft Room. 'Our timing is excellent,' he whispered, 'they've reached the end of Act One.'

Miranda was speaking to Ferdinand.

> 'My father's of a better nature, sir,
> Than he appears by speech, this is unwonted,
> Which now came from him.'

Prospero ignoring Miranda and Ferdinand strode downstage towards Ariel.

> 'Thou shalt be free
> As mountain winds; but thou exactly do
> All points of my command.'

Lorraine Jefferson, the stage manager, closed her prompt script then jumped up to face the actors sitting behind her.

'It's 12.30, folks, let's break.'

Prospero's voice was heard loud and clear over the ensuing chat. 'I have another line, Lorraine, or haven't you read the play yet!'

'Well, well, well,' murmured Vivian. 'What's up with Joshua, he's not usually so touchy.' He moved swiftly towards the acting area. 'Half a minute folks, I'd like you

18

to meet James Byrd, a management consultant who will be with us for a couple of days helping us to cut costs.'

There was a good natured laugh as they all eyed the superintendent still standing by the door.

'Come in, sir,' said Prospero, 'we'll not eat you.'

'Nor I you,' smiled Byrd.

The management consultant kept his eyes on Janet Shaw as she picked up a red shawl and draped it round her shoulders. With her long, fair, curly hair and blue-grey eyes she made a stunning Miranda, but Vivian was right, she looked as though she'd overdone the slimming business.

'Janet and Josh would you care to join James and me for a beer and sandwich at the Dirty Duck?' asked Vivian.

Janet looked a bit startled. 'I . . . I had planned to . . .'

'Whatever you've planned, love,' said Josh, 'cancel it and come along with us.'

For a few seconds she looked lost, a child at a new school now knowing what to do. Finally with a ghost of a smile she nodded her head.

'OK.'

Josh put his arm round her. 'Come on, Miranda, you look as though you haven't eaten for days. Come and get stuck in.'

She pulled the shawl more closely round her shoulders and allowed herself to be propelled by Josh towards the door. Vivian and Byrd followed them down to the pub.

Everyone in the company knew the drill. A table in the window was always reserved for Vivian who invited two or three members of the cast to join him in order to discuss any personal difficulties they were facing with characterisation or interpretation. An invaluable hour for most of the actors, but not for Janet as Byrd soon realised. He learnt a great deal about Josh who'd been with the company in London and Stratford for five years, but all he managed to glean from Janet was that she'd been with the company for eighteen months and had lived in a one room flat in the Warwick Road before moving into the terraced house left vacant by Sally Siddons.

At long last Vivian said, in scarcely more than an aside, what he'd been trying to say for days.

'Janet, do see the company doctor. He'll give you a tonic or at the very least some vitamin pills.'

'I've told you before, I'm all right,' she said tight lipped.

'But you've lost pounds and it's beginning to show in your face.'

'Make-up's a great transformer,' she said without the hint of a smile.

'But make-up will not give you energy, my dear. Come on, have another smoked salmon sarnie, fill those aching voids.'

'No,' she said firmly and that was the end of the matter.

Suddenly she got to her feet. 'Excuse me, Vivian, I've just remembered something.' She plonked £3 down on the table. 'That's my share.'

'Dammit, Janet, I don't need that . . .'

But she was gone.

'It's no good,' said Josh, 'You can't do anything for her. We've all tried. She hardly talks now, just twiddles some damn stones round and round in her hands while she's waiting for her cue. She's also taken to wearing heavy baubles round her neck. She's changed Vivian. When we started rehearsing we had a great rapport, I really felt she was my daughter. Now she could be a stranger from another planet.'

Through the window Byrd saw Janet cross the road and walk back towards the theatre. A figure rose from one of the tables outside the pub and ran after her. Josh followed his gaze.

'That's Lorraine, our hyperefficient stage manager.'

'The best we've got,' said Viv sharply. 'At least she's keeping an eye on Janet, for which I'm grateful.'

'Tell her, will you Vivian, that it's about time she learnt not to cut an actor off in mid-flow.'

'Come now, Josh, there's no need for such aggro. One line that's all you had to say.'

Josh frowned. ' "Come follow. Speak not for him", or should we say her?' he asked sarcastically.

'Mr Pryde,' said Byrd, as a thought flashed through his mind.

'Oh, for heaven's sake, drop the title, life's too short . . . Josh is good enough for everyone else.'

'All right,' said Byrd quietly. 'In *The Tempest* you're playing Miranda's father . . . didn't I read in the reviews last year that you played Capulet, Juliet's father?'

'Yes. Yes, I did. Ironic isn't it, two of my young daughters undergoing a personality change, and nothing whatever to do with the menopause. When the play opens Juliet is a disobedient fourteen year old.'

'And you,' said Viv staring at Josh, 'were the cantankerous father.'

'Christ! You're not suggesting, are you, that I'm the catalyst, the heavy father who turns his daughters out of house and home?'

'As I remember, Capulet uses strong words when addressing his daughter,' murmured Byrd.

'He does,' agreed Viv remembering every intonation Josh had used . . .·

Hang thee, young baggage! disobedient wretch!
I tell thee what, get thee to church o'Thursday,
Or never after look me in the face.
Speak not, reply not, do not answer me;
My fingers itch. – Wife, we scarce thought us bless'd
That God had lent us but this only child;
But now I see this one is one too much,
And that we have a curse in having her.
Out on her!

'Oh my God,' moaned Josh, 'It couldn't possibly have affected her. Could it?' he asked miserably.

'We'd need a psychologist to tell us that,' said Byrd softly, 'but I don't believe you were instrumental in her sudden departure. It may have been the wrong play for a young woman facing insuperable problems, and Capulet's words, not yours, may have been the breaking point.'

21

Josh shook his head. 'You don't know how I felt as Capulet. I was her father . . . angry . . . disillusioned . . . hardly able to keep my hands off her . . . threatening to disown her because she, my daughter, all but fourteen years old, was refusing to marry Paris. Paris an attractive, well-to-do, personable young man. I'm a Capulet. There's no way I'd allow my daughter to marry an enemy, a Montague.'

Byrd took a deep breath. He'd watched this small middle-aged effeminate actor with watery eyes turn into an outraged father over half a lager and a smoked salmon sandwich. Dealing with actors, he realised, wasn't going to be easy. Split personalities, but not in the accepted sense.

'Excuse me,' said Josh abruptly. 'I need some fresh air.'

He was gone before either of his companions could utter a word. They watched as he turned right out of the Dirty Duck, not back to the theatre as Byrd expected.

'Damnation!' yelled Viv. Not one head turned in his direction. They were used to his theatricality. 'It's going to be another disastrous rehearsal. I'll be spending precious time holding my fire, pacifying the pair of them . . . restoring their confidence.'

'It's a strange world, thought Byrd, in which an actor at the top of his profession, who's practised his trade for twenty-five years, needs moral support.

Josh Pryde, bearing his burden of guilt, sat on a bench in Holy Trinity Churchyard gazing at the shadows cast by the tombstones. He'd noticed too late that Sally Siddons had problems. At the time he was totally engrossed in his own part, had to be, it was the only therapy he knew. Young Ben had left him, not for someone else, he could have understood that, but because he wanted to travel. And not one word from him . . . not even a postcard saying 'Wish you were here'.

He heard laughter as a group of sightseers left the church. They passed him still laughing as though life

22

were an endless comedy. Never a comedy, he told himself savagely . . . it's one long ghastly farce.

They were Americans and their hilarity annoyed him. They wouldn't laugh at night in this spot. No one ever walked here alone after dark. Actresses returning to their digs always scuttled past in twos, never alone, not since the horrendous killing a few years back when a young woman was found mutilated, hacked to death. When Sally vanished this was the first place that he and Nigel had searched. Nigel sobbed on his shoulders, he remembered their closeness, and the hot wetness against his cheek. Sally had ejected her lover but he was still besotted with her, had never got over it. Only on stage as Mercutio had Nigel come to life, he was months coming to terms with a loss he couldn't understand.

Playing Capulet was never quite the same without Sally. The rave notices he'd received from *The Times*, the *Guardian* and the *Observer* had dwelt on the father–daughter relationship. He sighed, a week later they might not have been so kind. Sally's replacement was a wonderful comedienne in roles demanding a zany way-out approach but the intrinsic magic was missing. She neither sounded nor looked like his young daughter.

Josh tried to shake off his despair by wandering round the church before sitting in his favourite corner, but he saw only Ben's face and heard only Sally's voice. Ben, with his irrepressible Liverpudlian humour would have laughed him out of this dark mood. Even the lighting crew admitted to missing the jester, that's what they'd called him. He could make anyone laugh, but most of all it was his penchant for haunting travel agencies which had amused both players and technicians.

Josh hadn't bothered to clear up the small spare room in his flat. It was as Ben had left it. Untidy. Full of brochures and leaflets on travel, railway timetables, schedules from every major airline, brochures extolling coach tours, walking holidays, horse riding in Wales, activity weekends, package deals. He'd so much literature he could have opened a travel agency, but no one in the company ever believed Ben would leave. They'd made the mistake of treating his wanderlust as a joke, thinking he'd never have the wherewithal to travel round the world seeing Tibet, the Great Barrier Reef, the Sphinx, the Northern Lights and Niagara, but Ben had had the last laugh. He'd gone.

'Where,' asked James Byrd, looking round the Dirty Duck, 'are the rest of the cast?'

'Most of them will have snatched a sandwich and a coffee in the green-room canteen before finding a quiet spot by the river or in the Theatre Gardens.'

'Mind if we take a look?'

'OK. We'd better get moving, the afternoon session starts in ten minutes. The two bearded men made their way across the road and through the gardens where, sitting on a bench alongside a tall hedge, they noticed a happier looking Janet holding hands with Lorraine.

'So that's the way the cookie crumbles,' said Byrd.

'It's not what you think,' said Viv leading the way. 'Lorraine can ruffle Josh's feathers – does it for kicks – but like a good stage manager she also pacifies actors, solves their problems. I wouldn't be without her.'

The canteen run by Bertha, a rosy faced woman who mothered them all, was smaller than Byrd expected. As they entered the room they were assailed by the reverberations of Gerald's gutsy laughter. He was sitting with his back to them chatting to a young man in his early thirties, with a shock of carroty red hair, whose heavily tinted spectacles obscured his eyes.

'Gerald,' yelled Viv, who had to shout to be heard, 'when you've stopped laughing at Lenny's latest *bon mot*, introduce James to the man who's so profligate with our lolly.'

'You must be an accountant,' said Byrd smiling.

'No, electrics,' retorted Lenny.

'James Byrd,' said Viv as he made for the door, 'is merely another actor on life's mortal coil with a script open to a myriad interpretations. Answer his questions and he'll love you.' Viv winked at Bertha as he went.

'I'm no actor,' said Byrd, 'and I'm at a loss to understand exactly what "electrics" entail?'

24

'Lenny, our cheerful South Londoner, as no doubt you can hear, always hides his light under a bushel,' said Gerald. 'He's our chief lighting designer, an absolute magician, saves us the expense of bringing in whiz-kids from outside.'

'A magician! Perhaps I should investi . . . ' he stopped. 'Perhaps, you could tell me something about your job when Gerald has explained why I'm here.'

'He doesn't have to. News in a theatre travels faster than an avalanche down the north face of the Eiger. I don't think my job will help your enquiries, but give me an hour then join me in the lighting box.'

It was impossible through the dark glasses to read his expression, but he smiled back at the red headed magician. 'I'll be there.'

'James, I need some air,' said Gerald decisively. 'Why don't we walk round to New Place? The gardens are a riot of colour at this time of year and it'll take us less than five minutes. Give us a chance to discuss Sally in a more logical way. Viv has a vivid imagination, which is why he's such a brilliant director, but he's totally irrational over this issue.'

'New Place,' murmured Byrd, as they reached the gardens, 'This takes me back. I remember my old form master standing in the centre of the lawn castigating an eighteenth-century vicar who'd destroyed the mulberry tree Shakespeare planted because he couldn't stand the gawping crowds.'

'Worse than that. He also destroyed the house, the second largest house in Stratford, which Will bought from the Cloptons for sixty quid.'

'Weren't the townsfolk up in arms? And didn't the vicar have to leave?'

'They were and he left, but fortunately Garrick, reputedly, came to the rescue and planted a cutting from the original tree.'

'Reputedly! You mean it's part of the mythus?'

'Could be.'

'The garden looks the same as it did when I was a boy,' said Byrd, 'with the exception of that small mulberry tree in the centre of the lawn. I'm sure it wasn't there.'

'You're right. In 1969 Peggy Ashcroft planted a cutting from the Garrick tree, to mark Stratford's bicentenary festival. Her ashes were scattered here on a damp drizzly November day. The end of a spectacularly wondrous era. But you're here to discuss Sally. It's amazing how much we know about Shakespeare and how little we know about Sally.'

'But the mystery of Shakepeare's missing years has never been solved or that's what old Hedley told us.'

'That was 400 years ago, James. Sally left us a year ago after a two-year stint with us. We should have learnt a lot more about her. She had a generous and open disposition, never jealous, never malicious, consequently everyone loved her, yet we didn't know her.'

'That's why no one understood the change,' said Byrd softly. 'Sometimes I think it's easier to solve past mysteries than present ones.'

'You're back to the Bard?'

'Yes. Was he a pedagogue teaching young children in a stately home in Lancashire, or a clerk working as a petty conveyancer? Did he steal deer from Charlecote Park and run off to London to escape the consequences or did he merely join a band of strolling players? We'll never know.

'I can't think about the past. It's Sally's missing year that troubles me. For God's sake, James, find her – alive.

'We'll start at the top,' said Viv to the assembled cast. 'Do a run-through without interruptions, break after Act III for tea, and then continue to the end. OK Lorraine?'

'Yep. Maggie's on the book while I sort out Caliban's costume, and Alan should be here in a moment with a rough sound tape, mostly sea and wind, to provide a little atmosphere.'

'Which,' said Josh, in a stage whisper, 'she thinks is missing.'

Vivian ignored the jibe. 'Wonderful, Lorraine, you're always one step ahead.'

She grimaced to herself as she made her way to the wardrobe. Viv was not her favourite director, he was using her, knew she was the best stage manager around and as far as he was concerned that was her role in life. He'd not laughed openly when she'd pleaded with him for a chance to direct *The White Devil* in the Swan but his eyes had glazed over, said he couldn't spare her, said she'd need six months off to study the text. That was the end of the matter. She didn't even get a chance to say she knew it backwards in her sleep, had studied it for her degree course at Birmingham. Instead Viv had invited that niminy-piminy Geordie git to direct, the idiot boy who left out the dumbshow, an essential part of Webster's Jacobean melodrama.

Lenny unlocked the Control Room, and Byrd found himself in another space of surprisingly small dimensions, no wonder they termed it the lighting box. He'd imagined a large desk with banks of switches, the sort of equipment they'd used in the college theatre. The electrician, a man totally absorbed in his job, soon enlightened him. The entire lighting for the four shows in repertoire, and *The Tempest*, the next one to be added, were all programmed on one tiny computer.

'We have 500 lanterns out there,' said Lenny as he switched on the houselights and brought them up to full. 'Profiles, fresnels, front of house spots, floods, pageants, and a mass of ironmongery over the stage. We set up each play as it becomes part of the repertoire, taking care to double up on as many lights as possible, because we don't have much time between shows to re-set.'

'It's hard to believe,' said the policeman, as he looked at the small instrument with its red and green buttons, that your lighting control is contained in this toy.'

'It would be helpful, Jimmy, or are you James . . .?'

'Anything will do.'

' . . . if you don't discuss this toy, as you call it, outside these four walls.'

'Why's that?'

'It's new, the only one of its kind, invented by Michael Gibbs, and will eventually be marketed by Aurora, who have applied for the patent. We still have teething troubles, but it's light years ahead of anything else.'

Byrd laughed politely at his little joke.

'What sort of trial period do you envisage?'

'We've been experimenting for eighteen months, possibly need another six.'

'How can you be sure your own people won't talk?'

'They won't. They've been sworn to secrecy . . . we don't even mention it to the actors. Mind you they're not interested in the mechanics of lighting, all they're interested in is being in the spotlight.'

'Cynical!'

'It's their job, ain't it? If they want to keep working they've got to be seen.'

'Has there been a change of staff since the computer was installed?'

'Yeh. Ben's gone, but I only used him to check lanterns, clean lenses, occasionly operate a follow spot, and inspect chains.'

'Chains?'

'Yeh. Each lantern is secured to a bar by its own hook clamp, but by law there must also be additional chains as a precaution. Take a dekko, can't you see 'em?'

'Ah, yes.'

'They don't cost much if its a cost-cutting exercise you're doing.'

'I bet the computer cost.'

'Not a penny. It's a gift which has saved us a mint. Most of our outlay is on lamps, expensive items with a life of twelve hundred hours' roughly speaking, even the halogens. We replace lamps every day, and new regulations which came into force in 1992 mean all lanterns have to be tested.'

'That must take time.'

'Not really. All the lanterns have a bar code and we can check them using the computer. It's better than painting numbers on them which is what I had to do when I first came into the business and worked in one of the old Empires which housed travelling shows. We used to mark every bloody thing otherwise our lighting inadvertently vanished with the visitors, causing us problems the following week.'

'This lad you mentioned, Ben was that his name, where did he go and when?'

'The jester, that's what we called him. Ben Adams was a great kid. Always good for a giggle. However, he had the last laugh, mad keen on travel, you know, got wanderlust in his blood. Read every book on foreign parts he could lay his hands on, and, spent his spare time in travel agents picking up reams of bumph. The Arctic, the Antarctic, Timbuctoo, Hawai, Kurdistan, any place you like to mention he knew all about it. We never thought he'd go because he simply didn't have the lolly. One of those dreams, you know, that kids grow out of.'

'How old was he?'

'Twenty on the day he left.'

'And when was that?'

'Can't remember the exact date.' Lenny frowned and screwed up his mouth.

'God, I can't even call to mind the date Sally went missing. All I remember is Ben helping to set up the lighting for *Romeo* and then leaving before it opened.'

He looked at his visitor curiously, but said nothing.

Suddenly the sound of seagulls transported Byrd to a remote island. Birds swooped round the auditorium uttering raucous cries whilst tumultuous seas crashed against the rocks.

'Too bloody loud,' yelled Lenny as he switched on the intercom.

A deep throated chuckle was the only reply.

'I've someone with me Alan who can't wait to meet you.'

'Who's that? Madonna?'

'No. A management consultant who needs to know exactly how you budget and why it took you a week in Cornwall to make that tape.'

'Don't joke, Lenny, that's all I need.'

'Not joking. We're on our way.'

The sound equipment was housed in a larger area than the lighting. Again the policeman, thinking back to his college days, remembered they'd managed with a reel-to-reel Grundig tucked up in one corner of the lighting box. He was amazed at the enormous desk with its seventy-two ways which took up ten times more space than the lighting. A complete turnaround.

The sound engineer, a small man in his forties, stood aside for his visitor to get a better look.

'Why on earth do you need all this?'

'We can cope with anything thrown at us,' said Alan Hunt with a grin which stretched from ear to ear on his flat tortoise-like face.

'Good Lord, the actors aren't miked are they . . . not in this theatre?'

'Sometimes they have to be. Prospero would never be heard in the storm, so we give him a little more than moral support.'

'How did Shakepeare manage without all this gear?'

Alan grinned all the more. 'Can't imagine, but we do a lot more than the Bard's plays. We have to be prepared because Gerald is responsible for a short season between our main programmes which includes folk groups, jazz, opera, acts like Ken Dodd as well as the local operatic.'

A voice which Byrd recognised came over the intercom.

'Alan, you said the tape would be ready this afternoon.'

'It is, Lorraine. Thought you were picking it up.'

'Am I hell! Get on your bike.'

There was laughter in the background.

'Where is she?' whispered Byrd.

'In the wardrobe. That was Helen laughing.'

'Well, Alan, how long are you going to be?'

'Tell Viv I'll be five minutes.'

'Tell him yourself.' There was a click as she switched off.

Lenny laughed. 'Good old Lorraine, she doesn't change.'

Alan pulled a face, 'Not my favourite lady, too efficient by half.' The strident seagulls were abruptly cut off as Alan wound back the tape.

'I'd rather like to see the wardrobe,' said the police-man.

'No bother, matey. I'll drop you off, so to speak, on my way.'

Through the open door of the wardrobe Byrd could see two young women, with their backs to him, gazing out of the window as they ironed. The constant hum of washing machines made it impossible to hear what they were saying. A variety of stones and gems on the window sill caught his attention. Someone else, he thought, has Stephanie's craze for collecting. Every time they went on holiday his wife and daughter managed, despite his protestations, to load the car with stones. Strangely enough, eleven-year-old Kate could remember where they all came from. A prodigious feat of memory.

An older woman came into view holding a shimmering green leotard of enormous dimensions. She looked star-tled when she saw him standing there.

'Lost your bearings have you?' she shouted above the noise of the machines.

As he entered the room, Lorraine Jefferson, sitting riffling through a sketch book of costume designs, looked up.

'No, I don't think he's lost. Meet James Byrd, the sorcerer who's going to save us money . . . so make sure, Helen, you cut your cloth accordingly.'

'In the wardrobe that's all we ever do,' said Helen Franklin sharply.

The policeman held out his hand. The Wardrobe Mis-tress hesitated before grasping it as though it were a nettle.

'You're wasting your time in the wardrobe, Mr Byrd. We're extremely cost conscious. Not only do we reuse the basics but costumes once finished with are made available for hire. Wardrobe Hire which has recently moved to new premises is a business enterprise providing regular income throughout the year.'

Detective Superintendent Byrd got the message.

'I'm sure you're right. I'll try not to get under your feet.'

Helen Franklin relaxed. She'd made every effort to cut costs . . . sometimes it was very difficult . . . young designers once they'd crossed the threshold of the Royal Shakespeare Theatre though they had to be way-out . . . do a Reinhardt . . . use real leather when simulated material would do . . . silk instead of man-made fibre . . . design large hats which threw shadows across the face . . . create dresses in which no actress could move freely, and never never remember that dressing rooms were three floors up. She'd had to cope with them over the years but, as they discovered to their cost, she was no pushover.

'This garment here,' she said, spreading out the glittering green leotard, is the basis for Caliban's costume. The actor's lost a bit of weight recently so we're taking it in, and Viv who wanted the fish-like glitter thinks we've overdone it.'

'Which is what I said from the start,' said Lorraine bitterly.

Byrd wandered towards the window avoiding the two young women who were still ironing as though their lives depended on it. He gazed at the collection of stones before picking up a piece of rounded granite shot through with flecks of marble similar to ones Stephanie had collected in Anglesey.

'You into stones, Mr Byrd?' asked Helen.

'I'm not, but my wife is. She'd love these, particularly that piece of crystal. He held it up to the light where, in an instant, it became alive radiating all the colours of the rainbow and blinding him in the process.

'Where did you find this?'

'An Australian actor, who was with us for a season, gave it me. He said Aboriginals believe crystals are solidified light containing spirits. They even use them for medicine.'

'How?'

'By sewing them under the skin.'

'What a strange custom!'

Lorraine laughed. 'It's not new. In the sixteenth century Pope Clement's medicine was pulverised gems.'

'You're not joking, are you?'

'No. You should do some reading, Mr Byrd. You'll find crystals and stones have influenced us from time immemorial.'

'Are you all into stone mania?'

'Not too seriously,' said Helen, 'but it's interesting when we're making costumes to find out which stones were worn and why. As Lorraine said, you should read.'

'Not my scene, I'll leave it to my wife who could build a house with the rocks she's collected.'

'My two boys are as bad,' said Helen. 'There are so many stones in the fish-pond that there'll soon be no room for the fish.'

The Wardrobe Mistress surprised him. He'd looked at the hands of all the women . . . not a wedding ring between them.

'It must be difficult running a job of this magnitude and coping with a family.'

Helen nodded, but concentrated on removing sequins from Caliban's costume. You'd never understand, she thought, outsiders never do. It's not a job, it's my life, which is why poor Robert left and Mother moved in to look after the boys.

At last one of the automatons stopped ironing.

'I've finished the tunics, Helen.'

'Take them now,' said Lorraine quickly, 'and take Mr Byrd with you. Show him our luxurious star dressing-rooms.'

'Since when have I taken orders from you?' she snapped.

Emma the taller of the two girls stopped for a moment and grinned at Lorraine.

'She's off colour today, her boyfriend stood her up last night.'

'Liar! I was late leaving and by the time I reached the Garrick he'd gone.'

'Diddums,' laughed Lorraine.

'Why don't I give you a hand?' asked Byrd smiling down at Mary who was fair, short, and plump.

'Ta. You take the tunics and I'll bring the togas.'

He noticed that all the communal dressing-rooms were unlocked and costumes were hung on rails in the corridor. Mary looked at the name on each garment and checked names on dressing-room doors before hanging the tunics and togas on the rails.

'Are the dressing-rooms always left unlocked?'

'We rarely give actors keys, they'd lose them, but during the season the rooms are generally left unlocked because the wardrobe needs constant access.'

The newly promoted consultant followed her to the dressing-rooms reserved for leading actors. He strode into the first which he found unbelievably claustrophobic. With his bulk there was no room to move.

'My God! They can't be more than eight foot by six.'

'That's right. Five actors in each.'

'Not all together!'

She laughed for the first time. 'Of course not. Take a look at the legends on the door. You'll find the names of four actors and the titles of four plays. In a few days time *The Tempest* will be added and Prospero will also be in here taking his turn with Mark Anthony, Henry IV, Angelo and Orsino.'

'Well let's hope Angelo doesn't have a mental aberration and arrive on stage dressed as Mark Anthony.'

She giggled.

'They're lucky, Mr Byrd. The rooms are light and airy and overlook the river. They're in clover.'

'But how do five actors manage with one pin board for their good luck cards, photographs, and reviews?'

'It's no problem. Look, there are five boards hinged together which fold back on themselves . . . all actors have to do when they arrive is find the one which inflates their own ego.'

'If you don't care for actors why on earth do you work here?'

'Don't get me wrong. I love them because they're larger than life, never a dull moment.'

Byrd deciding to find his own way down to Gerald

Maitland's office moved swiftly along a third floor corridor, down three flights of stairs, and past the green-room. So far so good until he reached the darkened stage. He stopped halfway across the unlit wings . . . listening . . . knowing he wasn't alone . . . *no one here* he told himself but he clearly felt another presence . . . an unearthly sensation . . . then a vast crowd encircling him. It was uncanny, he could hear them whispering, generations of actors, hundreds of voices, but what were they saying? *It's my imagination, has to be . . . eerie . . . frightening . . . nightmarish . . . damn stupid too in a theatre. There's only one way to deal with fear . . . face it.*

Slowly he crept, unwillingly, towards the centre of the stage and looked out into the auditorium. A dim light emanated from the lighting box, and in that light he thought he saw a shadowy figure watching him . . . a figure which dissolved into the gloom . . . *damnation! I must get a grip of myself.* Gradually he was able to pick out the stalls and then the circle, but he couldn't escape the spectres that peopled the stage. He heard them strutting across the boards . . . the swish of skirts and then an awesome silence . . . seconds later a distant scream as swords clashed . . . then weeping . . . it was not hard to imagine bloody murders. He closed his eyes, *it's all an illusion . . . has to be . . .*

There was a slight sound upstage, and then a click as he swung round in time to see a watery light extinguished. *It's ridiculous to be afraid . . . there's nothing to fear in a place like this . . .* For a second he was rooted to the spot before resolutely moving swiftly towards the source of the sound.

There it was again, a slight click, but no light. He stopped, took a deep breath and moved towards the black tabs which he knew were there but couldn't see.

Suddenly he gave a shout as the floor beneath him vanished and he found himself hurtling into space.

He didn't hear the slight whirr of machinery. He didn't hear the hurried footsteps. His own voice echoing round the theatre was the last sound he heard until he opened his eyes, five hours later, in the local hospital.

Chapter 2

May all to Athens back again repair,
And think no more of this night's accidents
But as the fierce vexation of a dream.

Still half asleep he wondered why the bed was too hard and too small and why his left leg was encased in plaster. The last thought jerked him out of his comatose state as he clearly remembered the sequence of events before falling headlong into a black hole and losing consciousness.

He was hit by a great waft of 'Miss Dior' as Stephanie bent over and kissed his forehead.

'You've had a long sleep, James.'

'How long?'

'Five hours, give or take a few minutes.'

'I was set up. Set up within hours of starting the job.'

'Don't be silly, darling. You were a little careless, that's all.'

'Careless!' he shouted.

Nurse Atkins rushed towards the bed.

'Don't excite yourself, Mr Byrd. Not wise after such a nasty blow to the head. Relax, I'm sure Doctor Little will allow you home tomorrow.'

'What's wrong with my leg?'

'You've broken your fibula . . . it'll only take six weeks to heal.

'What!'

'There you go again. Be thankful it was a simple fracture. You must take things easy for a while, give it a chance to mend.'

'That's all I need,' he said bitterly.

'Darling, don't be so ungracious. Nurse Atkins is doing her best.'

'Is he always so cantankerous, Mrs Byrd?'

'Only when he's frustrated.'

'Men! They're all the same. There's another frustrated man sitting in the corridor, been there two hours waiting to have a word with your husband.'

'Sorry, Nurse,' said the abject patient, 'Please ask him, whoever he is, to come in.'

Viv Mollington, who'd cancelled his meeting at the Barbican, put his head round the door of the private ward.

'It's OK is it, Mrs Byrd, I won't be intruding?'

'No. Come and have a word while I ring home to let my daughter know he's alive and kicking – as usual!'

Byrd grinned at his wife.

'Love you darling, Kate too.'

Viv, on edge, wandered round the small room, not knowing how to begin.

'Sit down, man, you make me dizzy.'

'OK. OK. Look, James, I'm sorry. Someone will take the can back. It was unforgivable. Stage weights, when not being used, are always stowed away. Just one left in the centre of the stage by a thoughtless stage-hand did the damage tripping you up.'

Superintendent Byrd sat up.'

'Let's get this straight, Viv, I didn't trip. The stage was pitch black. Consequently I hurtled head first into a black hole.'

'But Lenny found you lying on the stage, with the working lights on. Perhaps' he trod carefully, 'concussion caused slight amnesia?'

'I am not suffering from amnesia. A slight blow on the head, that's all. I know exactly what happened. First of all the place was pitch dark apart from a dim glow in the lighting box. Secondly I distinctly heard muffled voices, and thirdly the click of a torch precipitated my move upstage across a gaping death-trap. You explain how that was engineered and leave me to find the assassin who tried to kill me!'

Viv knew there was a malevolent spirit at work. Perhaps John and Gerald would now take his misgivings seriously. Someone had wanted the policeman out of the way. It was

37

no accident. Byrd drummed his fingers impatiently on the bed table.

'Easy enough to set up,' Viv said softly, 'but how the hell did anyone know you'd be on stage at that particular moment? First of all he or she doused the working light in the wings. It's always on when we haven't a show because its a thoroughfare between front of house and backstage. The voices, I suspect, were recorded crowd noises which Alan may have been working on in the sound box.'

'No. I heard them on stage quite clearly.'

'In that case the speakers were operative. Ironically you referred to it as a death-trap. That's exactly what it was. A black hole created by a stage trap which had been taken down to its lowest level. Once you were out for the count the trap was raised to floor level and someone placed a stage weight alongside you. How's that?'

'Sounds feasible, but why didn't I hear the trap being lowered?'

'The hydraulic gear is well maintained, the sound would have been hardly noticeable covered, maybe, by the voices you heard.'

'So, to get me upstage the murderer clicked a torch on and off knowing I'd investigate, knowing full well I'm a copper.'

'Yes,' said Viv dismally. 'Now you'll have to discard your role of management consultant and play yourself.'

'Not on you life. We'll assume only one person knows, we'll have lunch tomorrow, and continue playing the same game as before.'

'But you'll be on crutches, not able to get around for weeks.'

'Want to bet!'

'You really are a card. Unfortunately I have a business lunch tomorrow.'

'What's new? You discuss business all the time.'

'Yes, but tomorrow's important. I'm taking a sponsor to Hall's Croft.'

'That rings a bell . . . didn't a Doctor John Hall marry Shakespeare's favourite daughter Susanna?'

'Spot on. You should find time to take a look. It's

38

another Tudor edifice beautifully restored by the Birth-place Trust. Part of it serves as a private luncheon club and the rest is preserved as a museum with an excellent tea room.

'Lunch, perhaps,' grinned the invalid, 'the day after tomorrow!'

James Byrd waited until his visitors had departed before ringing Sir Charles Suckling at home on an ex-directory number he'd winkled out of Viv. Sir Charles, although sceptical about the danger facing his officer who'd nearly shuffled off this mortal coil, agreed to the proposed *modus operandi*.

When Stephanie learned, late the same evening, that Detective Sergeant Georgina Mayhew was collecting her husband from hospital at 11 o'clock the following morning and driving him straight to the theatre she blew her top. Both she and Kate had been looking forward to having an invalid in the house for a blissful two or three weeks. Shared pleasures like Scrabble, crosswords, jigsaws, and Trivial Pursuit had gone right out of the window.

Chief Superintendent Keaton didn't express sorrow when he learned of Byrd's untimely accident, probably because he didn't feel any, but he vented his wrath upon all around him when Sir Charles ordered Detective Sergeant Georgina Mayhew to the scene of an imaginary crime. Why the hell hadn't Byrd asked for Sergeant Quinney, his usual partner?

Mayhew, with several days owing to her, had decided to spend them in Edinburgh with her mother who was slowly coming to terms with 'widowhood.' That's what she termed her state after her husband moved in with his 23-year-old secretary, seven years younger than Georgina.

Sir Charles rang as she was finishing her packing. Another few minutes and she'd have been winging her way to the land of her birth. Thankfully she accepted her mission. It let her off the hook, no need now to feel guilty. Maybe her mother would be easier to cope with in a month's time. Even more so, if she could be persuaded to come south and spend a few days in Oxford during the festival.

Nurse Atkins went off duty and Nurse Burrows, a buxom good natured woman with a broad Brummy accent, took over. She acceded to requests from the latest patient who showed no signs of settling down for the night. First notepaper, and a biro followed by endless cups of tea, and finally the use of a mobile phone for the night. He also insisted on hobbing, with the aid of a crutch, to the loo. Bottles and bedpans were not for him.

Shortly before midnight, after he'd made endless notes, he rang Bob Quinney at Kidlington with an unusual request. The sergeant, never surprised at anything his boss dreamed up, agreed to play ball.

Byrd then made a list of all the staff and actors he'd actually talked with during the four hours he was in Stratford. He eliminated the General Manager, Artistic Director, Manager-cum-Licensee concentrating first of all on Joshua Pryde, and Janet Shaw.

Had Josh made too great a show of playing the heavy father. Was it for real or was it a cover up? You could never tell with an actor. What exactly was his relationship with Sally Siddons? Not a jealous lover, that's for sure. Too effeminate, and too old. Not a jealous lover! My God! Am I going too fast? Perhaps Josh is besotted with Nigel?

Byrd's leg might be crippled but there was nothing wrong with his mind. He pondered over a possible relationship which could explain so much, but how did Josh engineer the scenario? How did he persuade Sally to eject Nigel? Did the whole sequence of events boil down to a *crime passionel?*

He then cast his mind over the technicians, Lenny and Alan. Something Lenny had said, which he couldn't call to mind, and then there was the maintenance wardrobe, a hive of industry, in which there was a varied array of stones. He'd feigned an interest in them but his attention had been drawn to the terraced cottage across the road in which Janet Shaw lived. He'd seen her enter at a time when she should have been at the rehearsal. She'd looked behind her as though she were being followed. Who would, he reflected drowsily, who would . . .

Nurse Burrows crept into the room and gazed down on an unwilling patient fast asleep with the light full on, notes strewn over the bed and his last cup of tea untouched.

Georgina ahead of schedule drove into the bay alongside the main doors of the hospital to find an impatient Detective Superintendent already waiting. She leapt out of the car to give him a hand.

'Get back, Sergeant,' he roared. 'Don't treat me like an invalid.'

She laughed, couldn't help it . . . she hadn't expected anything else. Byrd opened the nearside door, threw the crutch into the back of the car and eased himself into the passenger seat. Mayhew switched on the ignition.

'Relax, Sergeant, turn it off, we're not in a hurry.'

That makes a change, she thought.

'You need to be briefed, and from now on forget rank. We're management consultants. You've been brought in following my contretemps with a stage weight. That's our story.'

Georgina who'd only worked with the Superintendent on two cases knew he normally played everything close to his chest, never sharing all that he should with his team. She closed her eyes and listened. It was a rare treat to be fully in the picture.

'Now, Georgina, you know everything, but have learned damn all, so we'll start from scratch because despite my theorising nothing makes an iota of sense. How's your Shakespeare?'

'A reasonable knowledge of the tragedies, not keen on the histories, can't stand *Twelfth Night* which I did for O levels, but love *The Merchant*.'

'Why? Because Portia is a shining example of women's lib.'

'Never thought about it like that,' she said softly, 'though I wish the Chief would.'

'You'll get your promotion, Sergeant, I mean Georgina.

Solve this and the irascible Keaton won't have a leg to stand on.'

'Isn't that your problem, at the moment, James!'

He grinned.

'Before we get moving I suggest you unpin your hair, let it flow loose. Look like an actress, fit into the setting, get drawn into their world and share their fears . . . if any!'

They drove into the theatre forecourt parking alongside the Cavalier which had been left overnight. A girl in the box office who saw Byrd enter the foyer picked up the phone.

'He's here, Mr Maitland.'

James Byrd had thought the General Manager's office small, but it was a palace compared with Gerald's which contained two desks and a large filing cabinet leaving barely enough room for his two visitors to be seated. Gerald was amused to find a policewoman dressed in a brilliant emerald green shirt and red trousers looking more like an actress than many of the present company.

'Well, that's put the kybosh on that!'

'What's the matter, James?' asked Gerald.

'We need a desk, a phone, and a fax. I was hoping your office would be large enough to accommodate us.'

'You've no worries. John's one step ahead of you. He's spending the next two weeks at the Barbican and is not averse to his space being utilised.'

'Excellent!' said a more cheerful consultant.

Gerald handed them each a master key.

'You'd better have these torches too, if it's not bolting the stable door, and I'm sorry for what happened.'

'My own fault . . . "Nor heaven peep through the blanket of the dark to cry, hold, hold!" '

'You should play Donkey, James, you'd enjoy it.'

'Maybe I will.'

'At long last John and I have to admit that Viv is more clairvoyant than either of us. He's been right all along and we . . .'

'Gerald,' interrupted Byrd, 'have either you or John let slip to any member of the staff that I'm a copper?'

'No. We've been most circumspect. Nothing's been left lying around, no address, no telephone numbers. On my wall planner, as you can see, you're called the Platinum Consultancy.'

'Why?'

'My little joke, platinum being the best. Thought you might like the accolade.'

'Not until we've earned it.'

'Last night, James, you rang asking for plans of the theatre and company lists for both this season and last. They're all ready for you in John's office, and the coffee machine should be perking.'

It was and Georgina poured two cups of coffee and settled down to comparing personnel lists while her boss concentrated on the theatre layout.

It was possible, as he had thought, for any of the wardrobe staff to have reached the stage ahead of him via another route. He also suspected that the working lights, normally switched on in the prompt corner, could be overridden by a control in the lighting box.

'Got one!' yelled Georgina.

'Who?'

'A bloke called Ben Adams. He left six days before Sally Siddons vanished.'

'Ah, yes, the lad who wasn't initiated into the secrets of the new lighting board and who suffers from wanderlust. Any forwarding address?'

'No.'

'Where did he live locally?'

'At the same address as Joshua Pryde.'

'That's a turn-up for the book!' murmured Byrd.

Georgina's eyes glowed.

'Pryde is a brilliant actor. I saw him play Shylock in Edinburgh when I was at college. Heartbreaking, he was. On his final exit we saw a totally demoralised man. He used the same technique as Irving, so I was told. Having aged twenty years, he slowly walked towards the wings his arm held out. The last we saw of him were his drooping fingers, and total disintegration as his arm dropped lifelessly to his side.'

'Forego the imagery,' said Byrd testily. 'Let's concentrate on Josh. The fact that Ben lived with him may have put paid to yesterday's hypothesis. Would he have been chasing Nigel while he had Ben in tow?'

At noon Stephanie yawned as she closed the file she'd been working on feeling as if she'd completed a day's hard grind. She had, of course, because she'd risen at 5.30 a.m. to read for her Open Collegiate Law Course, breakfasted at 7.30 a.m., then dropped Kate at school at 8.30 a.m. on her way to Spratt and Salisbury's office in Oxford where she worked four mornings a week. By lunchtime she'd worked out how she could retrieve her husband's car from the forecourt of the Royal Shakespeare Theatre. There was a bus leaving Oxford at 1 p.m., she'd be in Stratford by 2 p.m.; time to drive the car home and get a lift back into Oxford to pick up her own car.

She rang James who sounded quite relaxed despite the fact that he hated personal calls when he was on duty.

'Hallo Stephie, you just finishing?'

'Yes. Are you OK, darling?'

'You don't have to worry, you know, it's not serious.'

'I know.'

'See you later then.'

'Not so fast, James, not so fast. I'm coming over by bus to pick up the Cavalier. You don't want to leave it another night, do you?'

There was a long pause.

'No. No . . . I've no intention of doing that. Bob Quinney is picking it up later this afternoon.'

'Great! What a blessing I rang.'

She slowly replaced the phone. What hadn't he been saying? She recognised the nuances, knew when he was being evasive. She shrugged it off. Get home and do some more reading. Forget about him.

The management consultants decided to see the last hour of the rehearsal before staging their own two-hander which, hopefully, would produce results.

'Tomorrow,' said Byrd, as they stepped into the lift on

their way up to the Ashcroft Room I want you to set up a trace on Ben Adams. No matter whether he's in Hong Kong or Honolulu we should be able to find him. While you're doing that I'll interview Mr and Mrs Siddons in Northampton. Find out why they're not creating mayhem about their missing daughter.'

'You forget, sir, you'll need wheels, we can't manage both jobs.'

'No problem. I'll be driving myself.'

'You're crazy!'

He laughed.

'Maybe I am, but Bob Quinney, who has automatic drive on his VW, has agreed to swap cars. All I need is a good right foot.'

Georgina was annoyed.

'If you're mobile, you don't need me.'

'Yes, I do. You may be able to get through to Janet Shaw. I can't.'

Viv wasn't at all happy to see Byrd and Mayhew creeping into a rehearsal which was proving traumatic. Nigel Fisher, suffering from smoker's withdrawal symptoms was playing Ferdinand like a zombie.

'We are,' said Viv through clenched teeth, 'playing a romantic drama. "Wherefore weep you?" must be full of concern, of love, making Miranda's reply all the more poignant. Let's try again.'

Nigel let out a deep sigh, took her hand in his, and looked into her large grey blue eyes with intense compassion.

'Wherefore weep you?'

Janet Shaw spoke the lines from her heart.

'At mine unworthiness that dare not offer what
    I have to give.'

'James,' whispered Georgina, 'do you realise what's happened?'

'No.'

45

'Janet's in love.'

'Good God! If you're right it's history repeating itself. And Nigel too?'

'Possibly. Think how she said dare not offer what I have to give. What's she actually saying?'

Viv glared in their direction. They got the message and said not another word until the end of the rehearsal.

As the actors collected their scripts, and Lorraine and Viv exchanged notes Byrd stood up and rapped the floor with his crutch.

'Don't be stupid woman,' he said glaring at Mayhew. 'You've only just arrived. There can't be any saving in either the lighting or the wardrobe. You go and see for yourself, and as for sustaining a company of this size, you're wrong again, it could be reduced.'

Georgina looked suitably crestfallen as Byrd, in high dudgeon, hobbled out. Several of the actors looked sympathetically in her direction, but it was Josh who approached her.

'We're going to unwind. Why don't you join us for a game of Donkey?'

'What on earth's that?'

When he had explained, she admitted her knowledge of Shakespeare was patchy but she'd love to watch.

Eight actors, and the stage manager remained behind to play the game, and, Daniel, the deputy stage manager volunteered to operate the music.

Sergeant Mayhew found it fascinating, never having realised how erudite actors could be. At the end of twenty minutes four players including Lorraine, Janet, Josh and Nigel remained. Nigel stood up on his chair and pointed at Lorraine.

> 'He is dead and gone, lady,
> He is dead and gone,'

She replied immediately.

> 'At his head a grass-green turf;
> At his heels a stone.'

Nigel grinned.

'Thought I'd got you there. Didn't know you'd stage-managed *Hamlet*.'

'I haven't!'

The game continued as the last two spoons were passed rapidly from player to player. When the music stopped Josh who was left without one immediately stood on his chair and pointed at Lorraine.

'The undiscovered country from whose bourn
No traveller returns, puzzles the will,'

My God, thought Georgina, he's thinking of Ben. Lorraine was quick.

'And makes us rather bear those ills we have,
Than fly to others that we know not of?'

Josh stepped down, removed a spoon and a chair muttering to himself, 'Don't know why we play with this lady, she always wins.'

The music continued as the last spoon shuttled back and forth between Janet and Lorraine. In their wild efforts to grab the spoon it fell on the floor. Lorraine dived for it and waved it aloft thinking she'd be the winner. Janet stood on her chair and in a quiet voice, which silenced the onlookers who seconds before had been enjoying the fun, said,

'O, I have passed a miserable night,
So full of ugly sights, of ghastly dreams . . .'

Lorraine looked up at her, astonished, and sat frowning as she tried to recall the following lines. At last, annoyed with herself, she gave in, and shook her head.

'Well done, Janet, you've won.

Josh and Nigel clapped which brought the slightest of smiles to Janet's lips. Georgina joined in the applause.

'Thanks everyone, I enjoyed that, it was great fun.'

Those weren't the words she used when later she described the game to Byrd.

'It was most revealing. They were getting at each other; a distinct undercurrent when it got down to the last four. Afterwards I had a cup of coffee with them in the green-room. I'm positive Janet is interested in Nigel, but I doubt whether it's reciprocated. Can't think why she wears those chunky stones round her neck, and continually fidgets with a bit of glass.'

'Glass!' said Byrd abruptly. 'That gives me an idea. Dash into the High Street and buy a couple of books on crystals, and runes.'

'What! Are you serious?'

'Could be nothing, but . . .'

'You're following your hunch as usual?'

'Yes.'

'On expenses?'

'Of course.'

She giggled.

'What's funny?'

'Just seeing Keaton's face if he ever checks through expenses and discovers one of his senior officers has been buying books on crystal balls. Something he wouldn't understand, James.'

The bookshop was busy but she found space in which to browse through a vast selection of books on tarot cards, palmistry, runes and crystals. She rejected anything scientific, and chose two describing crystals as natural transmitters useful in healing, meditation and magic. The smaller of the two outlined how to discover ones personal crystal, how to cleanse it and care for it, and its uses in telepathy and creative imagery. She couldn't see how any of this had anything to do with the case, but she'd have a stiff gin when she got home, put her feet up and while away the evening by learning about something totally outside her experience.

While she browsed, Byrd phoned. He called a Northampton number to make an appointment for the following morning.

Bob Quinney, who arrived after Mayhew had left for

home, had been ribbed on many occasions by Byrd for buying a second-hand car with automatic drive. With the tables turned he enjoyed demonstrating its easy manoeuvrability and comfort before swapping cars with a grateful boss, but much to Byrd's annoyance insisted on following him back to Bletchingdon. As soon as Sergeant Quinney had seen his precious B registration VW parked safely on The Green he doubled back to Divisional HQ making sure, before parking, that Keaton had left. He wasn't in the mood for explaining how he'd spent the last three hours of his day.

It was an unusually warm night for May, and Kate who loved eating alfresco begged her mother to have supper outside. Armed with a cloth and cutlery Kate sang happily as she set the garden table. Stephanie still feeling uptight about her husband working on a case with an attractive intelligent woman, not his normal partner, ran to the door when she heard the key being turned. She'd made up her mind to treat Mayhew as she would Bob Quinney and ask her to join them for supper, but she was overjoyed when she saw her husband standing on one leg beside the VW looking slightly apprehensive.

'Well ask him in, darling, I've cooked for four.'

'Ask who in?'

'Bob, of course, that's his car isn't it?'

'Yes . . . we've swapped wheels for a few days. His old boneshaker has automatic drive. I've an appointment in Northampton tomorrow. Need to be independent. Can't bear being fussed.'

Now she understood the reluctance to mention his crafty move over the phone. She wasn't angry as he'd expected. She was pleased that he was literally in the driving seat and not dependent on Sergeant Mayhew.

Kate came rushing down the stairs with a biro in her hand.

'Daddy, I want to sign your plaster, and you must get the actors to sign as well.'

'How,' he asked, trying not to raise his voice, 'did you know I was at Stratford?'

49

'I answered the phone when they rang to tell Mummy you'd had an accident on stage. Will you be going back there?'

'I might.'

'Then you can ask Nigel Fisher to sign. He's gorgeous, Daddy.'

'Wouldn't it be easier if I asked him to sign a programme for you?'

She gave a whoop of joy.

'Yes. Yes. Yes.'

'But not a word to your friends at school until the case is over.'

'Cross my heart, Daddy.'

Byrd fell back onto the sofa and put his foot up. It was swelling and itching like hell. He'd better do what the doctor ordered, and keep it horizontal for a bit.

'We're eating outside, Daddy, you'll like that.'

It was the last thing he needed with a swollen leg, but he couldn't spoil her treat.

Later that evening he listened enthralled while Stephanie expounded on crystallomancy. He'd no idea she was so well read on the subject.

'It's what I do with my time when you're not here. Read! Read! Read!.'

He got the message loud and clear. Quartz crystals, he learnt, were the most important stones being the base for the silicon chip, the miraculous root of twentieth-century technology. They were also good for the brain, for the soul, and dispelled negativity.

'That's only the tip of the iceberg,' said Stephanie. 'A myriad other stones work in a diversity of ways. Malachite aids the functions of the spleen; rose quartz produces compassion; zircon calms the emotions; jade increases longevity and fertility, and hematite copes with stress.'

'You don't believe any of this nonsense, I hope?

'I believe crystals can help all sorts of people with all sorts of problems, through auto-suggestion. Look at what a placebo can do. It's all in the mind, isn't it? But there's one crystal you'll never need!'

'Go on.'

'Garnet, or the 'Day Dreamer' stone.
'What does it do?'
'Enhances the imagination and balances the sex drive,' she said with a knowing grin.
'Don't give me ideas Stephie, nothing is impossible.'
'Do you want to prove it?'
'Why not!'

The Browns lived in Park Avenue, quite close to Northampton Golf Course, in a house they'd bought from the council soon after Sally finished at the Royal Academy of Dramatic Art.

Mrs Brown, who'd taken the morning off, was a secretary at a local middle school and Mr Brown whose hours were flexible, depending on the weather, was employed as Head Greenkeeper at the golf club. Mrs Brown, née Jones, who spoke with a strong Welsh accent, was scared. Her eyes said it all. She had expected the policeman to report that Sally had been found, and despite the fact she felt her daughter was still alive she feared the worst . . . there were unmentionable things that happened to young girls. She had not even dared to voice her thoughts. Mr Brown, on the other hand, said they'd never understood Sally who'd always done strange things, on the spur of the moment, ever since she'd been a little thing.

'I have this strong feeling,' said Mrs Brown, 'that she's suffering.'

'You have to understand,' said Mr Brown to the superintendent, 'that my wife's a Celt. She gets these strange fancies, in fact Sally takes after her. If you ask me, I reckon Sally scarpered with an attractive married man and is living it up.'

'Don't say that, George, I know Sally is suffering, even Father Maloney believes in telepathy. She is suffering. She wouldn't have gone off without telling me . . . she always needs . . . ' her voice broke' . . . I mean she always needed assurance.'

'Are you saying,' asked Byrd, 'that in some ways she's insecure and needs reassuring, and on the other hand she can make a hasty decision and carry it through?'

'Yes, you've got it. That's our Sal,' said Mr Brown.

'Were you aware,' Byrd spoke softly, 'of her lifestyle at Stratford?'

'Call a spade, a spade,' said Mr Brown abruptly. 'We knew she was living with Nigel Fisher. Isn't that what they all do nowadays . . . live with each other?'

'Nice young man,' said Mrs Brown. 'She brought him home, wanted him to see our little house, wanted him to see our background, not start off life on the wrong foot, that's what she actually said.'

'Did you know that she threw him out of the house?'

'We had heard,' said Mr Brown.

'Couldn't understand it,' said his wife. 'She was head over heels. He must have done something pretty dreadful to upset our Sal . . . she wouldn't . . .'

'Face it, Megan, she changed her mind.'

'So you say,' she whispered.

'Why don't you make Mr Byrd a cup of tea, love, while I show him Sal's room?'

He followed Mr Brown slowly up the stairs glancing at a wonderfully preserved icon on the landing. This was a ploy, he thought, to have a quiet word. He wasn't surprised to find the room in a pristine state.

'My wife dusts it every day, airs the bed, changes the flowers, dusts the icon.'

He buried his face in his hands and pressed his fingers hard against his forehead as if to dispel the images which he could never forget.

'Megan sits in here hugging Sal's old teddy bear. She doesn't want to face the truth.'

'And what is the truth, Mr Brown?'

'Who can tell? Originally I thought she'd taken off to get a bit of space. Isn't that what they say these days? But now, after a year, I think the worst. She's vanished off the face of the earth, like so many young women, like that Eversleigh girl whose mother's such a wonderful support to people in our position. But Megan won't ask for help. Says she knows Sally's still alive . . . says she'd know if she were . . . if she were . . .'

The policeman put an arm round the distraught man,

and sat him down on the bed. A man who suffered silently hiding his inner turmoil from his wife. Without asking, Byrd quietly opened the drawers of the dressing-table which were full of sweet-smelling underclothes, scarves, tights, and handkerchiefs. Finally he lifted the lid of a mahogany box decorated with mother-of-pearl.

'Her gran gave her that,' said Mr Brown, 'when she was a little thing because she liked the mother-of-pearl, the shiny bits she called them.'

He was disappointed. The box held all manner of odds and ends, a bone cigarette holder, a rosary, earrings galore, brooches, bangles, a string of cheap beads, and an old watch, but not a sign of what he'd hoped to find.

Mayhew followed in her master's footsteps. She spent an hour watching a rehearsal, visited the wardrobe, was shown round the sound and lighting boxes, and discovered that the working light on stage could only be operated from the prompt corner.

During the rehearsal Janet, when not performing, sat beside her at the back of the room. Several times she turned to stare, first at Mayhew's profile which reminded her of Jackie Kennedy, and then at the gem she was wearing. The crystal looked at its best against Georgina's black T-shirt, and from time to time she took it off the chain, held it tightly in her hand and closed her eyes.

She was about to leave thinking her actions had been in vain when Janet touched her gently on the arm, and whispered,

'Would you like to have a bowl of soup at my place during the lunch break?'

'That would be great, but where is your place?'

'Across the road. Number 33. The yellow curtains. I'll leave them closed.'

Georgina rose, but another gentle touch and another whisper.

'Don't let anyone see you!'

Gerald Maitland appeared at the door of the consultants'

temporary office at 11.30 a.m. precisely, as he said he would, carrying records of staff who had left the previous year.

He was far more interested in Mayhew than in the records. Why was this gorgeous brunette walking free? Byrd had been amused by the manager's curiosity on the previous day. Gerald, had at least gleaned, that she was a divorcee, lived in a flat in Kidlington, had given up a comfortable house by the river in Oxford and had got shot of a bank manager husband.

'You'll be wasting your time,' Byrd had said. 'She needs promotion more than she needs men.'

Gerald had never been interested in give-away women. He liked them gift-wrapped and difficult to open.

'What can you tell me about Ben Adams?' asked Mayhew in a voice which sent shivers down his spine.

'Ben. Ah Ben! He was one hell of a character. We called him the jester because he was always cheerful, always joking, would do anything for anyone, well almost anything . . . ' he stopped. A stupid thing to say.

'What do you mean, *almost anything*?

'Not fair to elaborate. I've no idea what went on behind closed doors.'

'You're talking about his relationship with Joshua Pryde?'

'Yes.'

'Well, why not share your thoughts?'

Those dark liquid eyes bored into him demanding an answer.

'I'd have put money on Ben being heterosexual, and we all know Josh's proclivity, so how they co-existed in the flat is anyone's guess.'

How on earth, she wondered, *will I ever find out?* Gerald laughed, as if reading her thoughts.

'Josh is a depressive, drinks a lot after the show, talks a lot too.'

'Thanks for that. Now tell me about the drill when anyone leaves?'

'Pretty much the same as anywhere else. If the technicians ask for a reference we give them one, plus a P45, pay

54

them up to date, and any accrued overtime is forwarded or paid into their bank.'

'How much could a chap working long hours hope to accumulate?'

'How long is a piece of string? We all knew Ben was trying to save, but I doubt whether there was much in the coffers because he was too keen on squash and martial arts, and they cost.'

'Do you know anything of his background?'

'Not a lot, except he hailed from Merseyside.'

Gerald quickly thumbed through the personnel file until he found what he wanted.

'Doesn't help I'm afraid. Only his Stratford lodging, and no forwarding address. He has £22.50 overtime outstanding. If you find him Georgina, tell him we owe him!'

Gerald returned to his office wondering why he hadn't asked the delicious Mrs Mayhew to lunch at Hall's Croft.

Mayhew left the office at the same time as the rehearsal in the Ashcroft Room came to an end. She stood at the entrance to the car park keeping an eye on the small terraced house with yellow curtains. Suddenly a figure darted across the road as though the hounds of hell were snapping at her heels. Georgina swiftly followed.

'Quickly,' shouted Janet, 'get inside.'

Once they were inside the sitting room which was in semi-darkness she peered through the curtains before turning on the light. Georgina wondered whether living in the same cottage as Sally Siddons had affected Janet.

'Mrs Mayhew could you manage home-made soup, or are you allergic to fungi?

'The name's Georgina, and mushroom soup sounds great.'

'OK. Make yourself at home while I fiddle in the kitchen.'

The policewoman gazed at the Magritte print over the mantelpiece and then stood transfixed at the collection of gems arrayed on an occasional table by the window. She'd expected to see one or two but not such a colourful collection, must be a dozen in all. *Was Dickybird's hunch right? Were gemstones part of the story? Fetching it a bit far*, she thought, *to connect them with Sally's disappearance!*

In the centre of the table there was a large chunk of natural quartz embedded in granite. She stood contemplating it, wondering how many millions of years it had taken to reach that state. A quiet voice behind her brought her back to reality.

'It's a bit dusty and hasn't yet been charged.'

Twenty-four hours earlier Mayhew wouldn't have understood the significance of the remark, but thanks to Byrd's intuition she'd read up on the subject.

'You won't need that fabulous centrepiece. Your other gems look immaculate and cared for.'

Mayhew didn't have to turn round to see if she was on the right track. Janet Shaw sighed with relief.

'I knew you'd be on the same wavelength. You're telepathic, aren't you? That's why you wore the crystal . . . a signal that you'd help me.'

Only then did Mayhew turn and look into Janet's eyes which mirrored her distress. She put an arm round her.

'Let's have that soup, shall we? It smells good.'

Damn! It was the wrong move. She felt Janet stiffen slightly . . . the moment of truth had passed. During the next hour she worked hard to repair the damage and retrieve the fragile relationship. By the time they'd finished eating the young actress was beginning to open up again. The policewoman trod carefully.

'It must have taken you years to collect all those gems.'

'No. No, it didn't. I found them.'

'Found them!' She took a quantum leap. 'They belonged to the previous occupant?'

'Yes. Sally Siddons,' she spoke so softly her words were difficult to catch.

'Why weren't they removed with her belongings?'

'She hid them, but meant me to find them.'

'But where in such a small house?'

'You must know, otherwise you wouldn't be sporting a crystal.'

Georgina gambled.

'They were buried.'

She said it with absolute conviction, then held her breath.

'Yes, you're dead right. It's an odd thing but I knew nothing about crystallomancy until I moved into this house. Finding Sally's note opened up a whole new world . . . and . . . and . . .'

'Yes?'

'I'm not ready for it. It's like making an act of faith . . . a leap into the dark. You seem so mature, so relaxed . . . I thought, perhaps, you might help . . . Mary's no good at all . . .'

'Mary?'

'She's wardrobe. Works with Helen. Mind you there are several others playing around, one or two seriously.'

Mayhew kept quiet not wanting to disturb the flow.

'It was meant, wasn't it, finding Sally's note? It could so easily have been destroyed when the place was cleared after she vanished.'

The word *vanished* upset Janet but she managed to control herself.

'Mary found it, a bit of luck really. She sat on the easy chair you're in when a load of coins spilled out of her pocket down the sides of the seat. She found the note while she was rootling around trying to recover the money. It was quite short.'

'Have you still got it?'

'Yes.'

As Janet moved towards the bookcase there was an angry knocking at the front door which shook the house.

'I'll go,' said Georgina.

'No. Don't. Keep quiet. She mustn't know I'm here, mustn't know I'm talking to you.'

Janet was hysterical. The knocking had the effect of producing the nervy agitated creature Byrd had described.

'Calm down, Janet. Please calm down.'

What on earth could she do to stop the girl shaking with sheer terror.

'I know,' she said, suddenly inspired, 'Why don't you

lie on the floor, and let me place the amethyst quartz at your head?'

Remembering the instructions that all crystals with magic properties have to be kept scrupulously clean she grabbed a piece of kitchen roll. Carefully she picked up the gem and placed it on the floor. Some minutes elapsed before she was able to cajole the frightened girl into lying down.

'Now do your normal relaxation exercises. A full breath, fill your diaphragm, then expand the breath through your chest up to your shoulders in one movement. You know how?'

Janet nodded. There was another onset of furious knocking. Janet shivered, but calmed down as Mayhew placed a hand on her forehead. She breathed in.

'Now hold your breath for four and release it slowly to a count of eight. Do it again and again.'

The knocking subsided leaving only the sound of Janet's deep and regular breathing. The girl who minutes before had been frantic lay totally relaxed. It was only then that Georgina remembered the rest of the drill she'd read the night before.

'Now visualise your amethyst spinning gently above your head. See the light spilling out like a great waterfall dowsing first your brow, your face and your whole body with soothing relaxing energy. Flood your aura until you are immersed in a sea of amethyst light.'

Mayhew was amazed. All these extraordinary instructions had proved efficacious.

The patient opened her eyes and as she looked into Georgina's troubled face she smiled.

'Thank you . . . you're a wonderful lady.'

Georgina whispered, not wanting to break the spell, 'Shouldn't you be at rehearsal?'

'They're doing Act II. I'm not called until . . . until . . . until . . .'

Prospero's daughter fell asleep on her own island of doubtful magic.

Chapter 3

The uncertain glory of an April day,
Which now shows all the beauty of the sun,
And by and by a cloud takes all away!

Two police officers playing out their roles of management consultants sat in their temporary office exchanging notes. Byrd, unusually for him, mentioned every detail, including a joke letter addressed to Sir George Brown which the postman had handed him as he rang the bell at 186, Park Avenue North.

Sally's father had glanced at it without comment, not a glimmer of a smile, and left it sitting on the hall table.

'Knights don't have to live in castles, James.'

'Don't be facetious, knights of the realm are hardly likely to be greenkeepers and live in council houses.'

Mayhew, also with total recall, described the two hours she'd spent with Janet Shaw behind closed curtains.

'You slipped up, Georgina. You should have come away armed with the note, so conveniently found, stuffed down the side of a chair.'

'You don't understand, sir,' she said through tight lips. 'To return to the business of the note might easily have upset a fragile relationship. Someone out there scares her rigid. I wouldn't be surprised if she knows what happened to Sally Siddons.

'Where's the note?'

'She was making for the bookcase which holds a couple of hundred books. Could take an age to find, even supposing we can get in.'

'I'm not proposing breaking and entering, but Gerald will have a spare key, and a periodic check of the property wouldn't be out of order.'

Byrd was irritated. He needed to compare Janet's note with the one Viv Mollington had received. *I go now of mine own accord. Look not for me.*

'Get in there, Sergeant, as soon as possible.'

He couldn't understand what was wrong. Mayhew, usually so calm, was distinctly uptight. She gave him a look which would have quelled a lesser man.

'Come on, let's be having it.'

'I spent two exhausting hours with Janet listening to the story of her life. She's scared, but not stupid. I thought she'd rumble me. It was like treading a high wire without a safety net, something you wouldn't appreciate. Three years ago her parents and sister were all killed in a horrendous coach accident in France. She can only escape the ghastly images when she's fully immersed in a role. She desperately needs help, something to fill the emptiness. She didn't mention Nigel, I'm sure she's in love with him, but for some reason she can only communicate through the play. Let's hope he feels the same way,' she said despondently.

'But yesterday they weren't dissembling, they were expressing their love for each other. What's changed all that?'

'We're forgetting, aren't we, that actors can simulate any feeling, and what we saw or felt was in our minds. We saw Ferdinand clearly in love with Miranda?'

'My God, how do actors separate their actual life from their stage life when they're playing characters which totally absorb them?'

'Doesn't our job do the same,' said Georgina softly. 'We try to get into the minds of our victims and killers, and for weeks on end their lives have more meaning for us than anything happening on the home front. Our colleagues,' she picked her words carefully, 'are often more close to us than our family, mentally, I mean.'

'The crucial test at the moment,' said Byrd abruptly, 'is are you on Janet Shaw's wavelength?'

'I'm getting there, but playing around with crystallomancy is something I'll never fully understand. There's even a magic mirror on the mantelpiece, which she may use for scrying.'

'And what the hell is that?'

'It's crystal-gazing basically, but can be done using a mirror.'

'We're getting into the realms of fantasy, Georgina.'

'Not as fantastic as you think. Queen Elizabeth didn't make a single decision without first consulting Dr Dee her court magician. It's said he warned her of the approach of the Spanish Armada, by using a black Mexican obsidian which Horace Walpole later called "The Devil's Looking Glass". He also used a magic mirror consecrated to an Egyptian goddess.'

'Elizabeth the First might have listened to her sooth-sayers, but not Elizabeth the Second. It's the stuff of fairgrounds and wandering gypsies.'

'I would have agreed with you yesterday, sir, but reading those books last night was an education. There are thousands of people who believe crystals can influence their lives, who actually derive power from the gems. If you'd seen Janet you would have understood. She's scared, but lying on the floor with an amethyst at her head calmed her down. I wanted to tell her it was a lot of bullshit, cradle her in my arms and dispel the fear.'

'Go easy, Georgina, don't become emotionally involved. It happens to us all,' he said ruefully thinking of his last case. 'Emotion impairs our judgement. You will help the girl by discovering why she is scared. Allow yourself to be a sounding board, try to be impersonal, and not a surrogate mother. The stage manager's keeping a watchful eye, leave it to her.

'But not Mary, the girl in the wardrobe who . . . ' she stopped. 'God! how stupid I've been.'

'Not stupid, Sergeant, just a little slow, perhaps!'

'It was Mary who stuffed the note down the side of the chair before scattering her money in all directions. Mary too, who could keep an eye on the house from the wardrobe, but it doesn't add up.'

'You mean small, fair haired, dumpy Mary could never frighten anyone?'

'That's about it.'

Mayhew left her boss checking Sally's personnel file for the umpteenth time while she went in search of Lenny. Ben was uppermost in her mind. There were some answers that only the men who'd worked with him closely could provide. She found the chief electrician in the green-room finishing off a game of Scrabble with Alan Hunt.

'Come and join us,' shouted Lenny, who at long last had got rid of his Q by putting down "QANAT".

'Qanat, what's that when it's at home?' asked Georgina.

'A pipe the Ay-rabs use for irrigation,' he smirked. 'Get the lady a coffee, Alan.'

'There's no need.'

'He can afford it, he's just won on the gee-gees.' He looked up at her with a quizzical expression. 'Take your weight off your feet.' He had an idea . . . wanted to test the water.

Alan good naturedly paid for three cups of coffee, and brought them over to the table where he sat fidgeting with the Scrabble letters as she questioned Lenny.

'Do you spend all your spare time in the theatre?'

'Yep. There's no point in going all the way home, and back again for the evening performances.'

'Where's home?'

'Edgbaston.'

'Why don't you move to Stratford?'

'Can't sell our flat, simple as that. Mind you in this business there aren't any gilt-edged jobs. In two months time I could be out on my arse and looking for work in the new complex in Brum.'

'Have you been here long?'

'Four years, a long time in a man's life, but Viv's a great guy, we see eye to eye so I reckon I'm good for at least another four years.'

Georgina laughed at the optimistic Cockney, but wondered why he'd even mentioned insecurity. She had the feeling he didn't expect to be in Stratford much longer.

'Wouldn't mind your job,' said Lenny. 'Different place

every week, meeting new people, asking awkward questions, raising the dust, and getting to hell out of it. Like it do you?'

Mayhew knew he was probing.

'Where's the Platinum Company based?'

'Oxford.' Damn he'd been in Gerald's office. Had seen the wall diary.

'Specialise in theatres, do you?'

'No. Our work covers a variety of venues. I go where my boss commands.'

'Where do you train for your sort of work?'

'Edinburgh University helped, but not as important as being streetwise and able to add two and two. There you have it.'

The phone disturbed their skirmishing.

'Message for you, Lenny,' shouted Bertha. 'There's a gent in the foyer waiting to see you.'

'Excuse me, Inspector.' Grinning he dashed out to meet his unnamed visitor.

'What the hell did he mean by that?' Mayhew was stunned.

Alan was slow to answer as he arranged the letters to read 'police inspector'. 'He gets these bees in his bonnet. He thinks you and the other chappie are coppers working on Sally's disappearance, thinks her parents have got moving, at last. Mind you,' he said softly, 'I wish you were. She was a smashing girl, we were all in love with her. Ben more than anyone . . .'

'Ben! Wasn't he the technician you called the jester?'

'Marco Polo would have suited him better, he'd really got the travel bug, or maybe he was just bored.'

'No one could be bored in a place like this?'

'Don't you believe it. Ben was a bright lad, but never allowed to get near the computer and he'd been reared on the damn things.'

'What do you mean?'

'His dad's a systems analyst and I reckon Ben could programme anything at the drop of a hat.'

'Where does his dad hang out?'

'Liverpool. He's a big noise with the Royal Insurance.'

Mayhew could have hugged him, never minding that the bags under his eyes and his lugubrious expression made him more tortoise-like than ever.

An hour later Georgina was singing to herself as she belted up the M6 on her way to Merseyside. She'd done her homework. Martin Adams, an executive of the Royal Insurance Company, was not in his office when she rang, but his secretary who failed to understand the meaning of her title was most forthcoming. Sounding adenoidal like one of the *Liver Birds* she told the caller where he'd been the previous day, where he was that day and where he'd be during the evening. That was all Mayhew needed. His home, she'd gathered, was in the Wirral tucked away on the outskirts of Thornton Hough, a commuter's paradise.

To avoid Liverpool she left the M6 at Junction 20 and took the M56 which linked with the M53 serving the Wirral. Thornton was a small village, but she had no difficulty in locating the black and white Victorian Gothic lodge. She parked in the drive between two Jaguars which said it all. There was no shortage of the ready in this household. As she walked towards the front door she caught a glimpse of a pale blue Metro, at least ten years old, which had earned its keep. The gardener's perhaps, or the housekeeper's?

The front door was opened by a short, dark haired, suntanned man dressed in jeans, and a gaily coloured shirt who looked vaguely Spanish and had bare feet.

'You must be Sergeant Mayhew?' His eyes twinkled knowing he was not what she expected.

'And you are Mr Adams?'

'Yes. Come in, Sergeant, you've had a long drive.'

She hesitated. Was he really a high powered executive?

'Well, don't hang about. Come in and join us for a drink. Your business can wait.'

Mrs Adams, also dark haired, dark eyed, and petite was in the sitting-room working away at a tapestry. She made no effort to get up but when she smiled at Mayhew her whole face lit up.

Husband and wife looked more like brother and sister. Mr Adams plied his guest with coffee followed by a glass of excellent Moselle which she hadn't the heart to refuse. Mayhew felt like a neighbour making a social call not a police officer on official business.

Ben's father may have been small, bare footed, and unlike any tycoon she'd ever met but he had inner strength and quiet authority which she found attractive. Mrs Adams, strangely incurious about an unexpected visit from the police, carried on with her gros point.

'Now, Mrs Mayhew,' said Martin Adams, as he replenished her glass, 'what is this all about?'

'Between these four walls I have to tell you you that I'm working on a case at the Royal Shakespeare Theatre in the guise of a management consultant.'

'You mean,' said Mrs Adams, 'that at long last something is being done about the disappearance of Sally Siddons?'

'Yes.'

'And,' said Mr Adams, 'you want to contact Ben who also vanished without trace.'

'Yes.'

'Where do they think he is?'

'There are many theories,' smiled Mayhew. 'The Great Barrier Reef, Nepal, Bali, Mexico, Hollywood, going down the Amazon, and that's just for starters.'

'He's always wanted to travel, ever since he was a small boy,' said Mrs Adams, as she concentrated on tramming a large pink rose.

'It's all in the mind, Emily dear. He never will,' said her husband with absolute certainty.

'What do you mean?' gasped Mayhew.

Mrs Adams laughed as her husband opened the door and shouted up the stairs.

'Have you a moment, Ben?'

Georgina closed her eyes. How stupid she'd been. Nearly missed the boat by assuming he was abroad. Only Alan Hunt's chance remark had led her to Thornton Hough.

'Hi there!' said the young man who, although taller and broader, resembled his father.

'Sit down, Ben. Sergeant Mayhew wants to ask you a few questions, or would you rather talk to her in private?'

'I've nothing to hide.'

He sat on the fender stool looking her straight in the eyes.

'Could you,' she said softly, 'tell me what you've been doing since you left the theatre, and your reasons for leaving?'

'Reasons for leaving!' He pulled a face. 'I had plenty of reasons for staying, but I simply couldn't stand it any longer. They all thought me a bit of a joke . . . I am, of course, but the one talent I have, which Lenny refused to recognise, is an ability to master any computer. Like my dad, you see. I was fed up at being treated like a menial, running along the catwalks cleaning the lenses, running errands, and if I was a good boy operating a follow spot.

Don't get me wrong, I love the theatre, but I wanted to be more involved, not treated like an imbecile. Staying with Josh helped. Everyone, except Sally, thought we were lovers, but we let them weave their fantasies. We were good for each other. Josh unhappy about his sexual makeup which he'd never come to terms with, and him listening to me me beefing about my role as dogsbody.'

Emily Adams pricked her finger as she stopped half way through the canvas to look at her husband. She was upset. Ben had never talked much about the old actor he'd lodged with . . . she'd no idea he was like that . . . Martin shook his head, no need to worry he was saying.

'He's a deeply sensitive man,' said Ben unaware of his mother's disquiet, 'who was hurt by the change in Sally. They had a wonderful rapport when rehearsals began, but it dwindled away until he couldn't get through to her, neither on nor off the stage.'

He sighed, and looked out of the window at the fountain spraying water over Aphrodite.

'No one has a pure motive for doing anything. The change in Sally upset me too. We were good friends, never anything else, never likely to be, for who would look at an electrician's mate when Nigel Valentino Fisher was around?'

Georgina sensed the bitterness, but held her breath knowing there was a lot more to be said.

'Not just Nigel, of course, there were others interested in her, but the thing that really got my goat was not being allowed to play around with the computer. 'It's hush hush', Lenny kept saying. Hush hush as far as I was concerned, but not for some of the visitors he took round the auditorium. However, I got the last laugh. Viv sent him down to the Barbican on a day when the assistant electrician was also off. One of them had left his key in the lighting box. Alan wasn't around so I grabbed the opportunity and spent three hours working it all out. Quite an amazing bit of equipment. Years ahead of its time.'

He shook himself, got up, wandered to the window and stared into space not even seeing Aphrodite.

Georgina sat quietly fidgeting with the gem she was still wearing. As Ben finally made up his mind to voice his thoughts about the computer he turned to face Mayhew and saw she was fondling the crystal. Suddenly his whole mood changed.

'Not you too,' he murmured.

'What's the matter, Ben?' asked Martin who felt the vibes but couldn't get the picture.

'Who are you?' yelled Ben.

'Go easy, son. Mrs Mayhew is a guest.'

'Is she? How do you know she's a police officer, how do you know . . .

He stopped as Georgina handed her ID card to Martin Adams. For some seconds Georgina couldn't understand the change in Ben's attitude, then she took off the crystal and waved it backwards and forwards like a pendulum.

'Is this what's bugging you?'

He nodded.

'It's not crystal, just a bit of polished glass, made in Korea I shouldn't wonder.'

'Sit down, Ben,' said his father, 'and share whatever's on your mind.'

67

He sat down slowly like an old man.

'It will sound daft, as stupid as science fiction, which it probably is.'

'Go on.'

'It all started, as a game I think. Several members of the company egged on by a girl in wardrobe used to meet and play around with crystals. At first Sally laughed, and used to tell me everything that happened during lunch breaks in the green-room. Nigel pooh poohed the whole thing, would have no truck with it, and went off to the Dirty Duck for a pint. Sally and I thought it would be a great joke to get Lenny in on one of the sessions. I'd gaze into the cluster of crystals placed in the centre of the circle, and tell him all the computer's secrets I'd discovered when he was in London.'

'You mean,' said Emily Adams, 'that they behaved like gypsies and read the future in a crystal ball?'

'Except,' said Martin quietly, 'it was a cluster, presumably in its original state after being hacked out of rock, like the pieces we saw in Snowdonia last year.'

'You've got it, Dad. The jagged pieces of quartz were still firmly embedded in slate. Lenny had agreed to join the party when Sally, for some obscure reason, got cold feet. She'd always joked as she explained the theory behind crystal gazing, but one day she began treating it seriously, and told Lenny not to show his face. I'm sure she believed that by wearing a crystal she was attuned to Mother Earth, and her life would be transformed by harnessing the energy of a living spirit. A living spirit in a bit of quartz! Can you imagine anything more crazy?

Sally was a successful actress who didn't need help, whose natural talent would have taken her right to the top. She didn't need bits of glass for moral support. She told me her crystal was physical, that she could hold it in her hand, increase the link between mind and matter, and focus her own energies in a new direction. Codswallop, and she believed it!' He was almost crying with rage. 'She actually washed the damn thing in the sea on a night when the moon was waning. She knelt down on the shore, and thanked the spirit of the sea for releasing her from all the darkness within her life.'

'What darkness?' asked his mother.

'I'm not sure. She said she was lost and lapsed whatever that means.'

'Good Lord! Was that last year when you brought her up here? The night you were late back from Heswall?'

'We were late because she paddled in the sea and washed the bloody thing in water where you and I wouldn't even swim. It was the last time we were ever together.'

Georgina feeling sorry for the young man tried a different tack.

'When you left Stratford they all thought you'd gone abroad and were living the life of Riley in Hawaii or sailing up the Amazon. Where did you go?'

Ben grinned.

'I collect travel brochures like other kids collect stamps.'

'You can say that again,' said his mother. 'You should just take a peek at his bedroom!'

'So you didn't leave this precious isle?'

'No. I'm pretty good at sport and fancied a stint in a leisure centre, for a change. There was a vacancy at the one outside Chester so I went along and before applying chatted up a couple of the sport attendants. It sounded good, would have suited me to a T, but I put my foot in it when one of the lads asked me where I'd been working. Their reaction was instantaneous. They looked at each other and laughed themselves silly. "Know a Lorraine Jefferson?" asked one. I had to admit that I did. It didn't take them long to fill me in about Lorraine's six-month stretch at the centre where she'd been Entertainment Officer.

Thought she was God's gift, apparently; they said she arrived spouting all the jargon that's peculiar to arts officers. She'd come down from university with an honours degree in drama and English literature which she mistakenly thought had prepared her for acting and directing, but at Chester her job was to arrange a series of events ranging from pop groups to classical concerts.

The first concert given by a Polish Orchestra was a near disaster. The concert manager arrived with his band of 110 players to find that only 70 seats had been set out on stage, and was even more astonished to find she'd put the conductor and soloist into a communal dressing-room with the players. There was no rostrum for the conductor and to compound the problems she'd not arranged teas for their mid-rehearsal break. The manager of the centre pacified them and dealt with the situation. I'm told she had absolutely no gift for coping with artistes and their problems.

It was even worse when a travelling company arrived to perform Ibsen's *Master Builder*. She saw a rough rehearsal and then proceeded to tell them how it should be acted, not realising they were doing a walk-through and saving their energy for the evening.

News travels in the entertainment biz and I knew everyone would be wetting their knickers if they heard I'd only travelled as far as Chester, not only that, there were a lot of people I wanted to . . . wanted to forget.'

'So where are you working?'

'At the Royal, of course. With Dad's mob. Suits me down to the ground. Computers may control us, and I may have to clean the VDU from time to time, but it's better than running along catwalks cleaning umpteen lamps.'

'So it's *your* blue Metro which has seen better days?'

He gave her a wicked grin.

'It is, but by the end of the year, if I don't go abroad, I aim to own an MGB.'

Mayhew left Thornton Hough knowing Ben had not said it all . . . knowing there were gaps, and what did he mean by Sally being lost and lapsed?

James Byrd had not been idle. To give credence to the job of consultant he'd driven down to the workshops to take a look at the carpenters and scene painters who were putting the finishing touches to the set for *The Tempest*. The backcloth, fully stretched on the paint frame, depicted a wonderful Turneresque sunset. Prospero's isle would be truly magical. The men knew who he was, no need to ask, so they kept on with their jobs expecting questions which never came while the silent inquisitor made notes.

It occurred to him whilst he was admiring their handiwork that if only he could talk to Nigel Fisher as a police officer he might make some headway. The constraints imposed by the role of management consultant were beginning to irritate him. It was a year since Sally's disappearance. Someone must know a lot more than they'd gleaned, and who better than Nigel?

As he drove slowly back to the theatre he caught a glimpse of the Holy Trinity spire, and on the spur of the moment decided to travel back in time. An hour's contemplation wouldn't come amiss.

It was blissfully quiet. Only two women were in the church and they were on their knees praying. He hobbled towards the choir stalls and was amazed to find a familiar figure sitting there, as immobile as the bust at which he was gazing.

'Good afternoon, Mr Pryde,' he whispered, 'isn't this taking Bardolatory to its limits and shouldn't you be rehearsing?'

The actor blinked several times before focusing on the unexpected figure of James Byrd.

'Viv,' he hissed, 'is concentrating on Miranda and Ferdinand's scenes, not before time, if you ask me, and as I've only a couple of lines Lorraine's reading in for me.'

Byrd sat beside him.

'Do you often worship in this shrine?'

'Worship? Never.' He looked up at the coloured bust of William Shakespeare. 'I spend long hours thinking about the injustice done to the greatest poet the world has known. I try to imagine what he was really like. This man who was described as "gentle", and who towered above lesser poets.'

'You must know him,' said Byrd.

'Through his words, you mean?'

The policeman nodded.

'No. I don't. No one does. Thousands of books have been written, millions of words uttered, but there's nothing that really reveals him as a person. We know as an

71

eighteen-year old he was probably forced into marriage. May have been unhappy, who knows! He certainly spent most of his working life in the great city, and never as far as we know took his wife and children with him.'

'Not an unhappy life,' said Byrd. 'Many of his plays are full of joy, they tell us a lot about the man.'

'Let's hope,' said Josh, 'that he found solace with the dark lady of the sonnets.'

'Happiness may have been elsewhere,' said Byrd remembering old Hedley's anger. 'Much more likely that he shared the bed of Mistress Davenant, the landlord's wife of an Oxford Tavern.'

'Legend, sir, pure legend,

'Not according to Sir William Davenant, who in his cups, always swore he was a poetical child.'

'You seem uncommonly clued up about the Bard.'

'I became engrossed as a youngster, and have continued reading ever since. I've many theories which don't fit mainstream opinions, and which would be laughed at by academics.'

'I should have thought profit and loss accounts were more in your line.'

Byrd ignored the gibe.

'When I visited this church as a boy I found it hard to believe that Shakepeare was actually interred here next to his son-in-law and daughter. He should be in Westminster Abbey in Poets' Corner.'

'That's the greatest injustice. No one rated him, then. He was a jobbing actor and writer who'd made a bob or two, enough to buy up properties and land and own one of the biggest houses in Stratford. But, sadly, it was fourteen years after his death before Milton spoke of him as a wonder.

> Thou in our wonder and astonishment
> Hast built thyself a live-long monument.

No one,' said Josh angrily, 'gave him full measure until Garrick appeared on the scene in 1769 and held the first Shakespearean Festival. Don't you see, Garrick put Shakespeare on the map for ever. London came to Stratford for the plays, for the fireworks, for the racing, for the feasting.'

The women who'd stopped praying found themselves listening to the outpourings of an actor who would never know the man he idolised.

'His bones are still here,' said Josh, 'because no one dared move them. Just you read that verse over there.'

Byrd moved nearer to the altar and read the plaque in front of the Bard's resting place.

Good friend for Jesus sake forbeare
To dig the dust enclosed heare
Bleste be the man that spares these stones
And curst be he that moves my bones.

'Come on,' said Byrd impulsively. 'Let's find ourselves a coffee.'

'We'll go to my place,' said Josh. 'There's a lot we haven't said.'

It wasn't Shakespeare Byrd wanted to discuss.

The apartment was what he'd expected. Two small bedrooms, kitchen-diner and bathroom, but the view was out of this world. Boats glided silently down the Avon towards Clopton's Bridge; swans and ducks in their natural habitat ignored the anglers and the traffic. They were happily being fed by an old lady who carried a large bag of goodies. They stretched, shook their wings, and one intrepid enough to haul himself up the bank stood alongside his benefactor who talked to him like an old friend.

'Decaffeinated suit you?' asked Josh.

'Indeed, yes.'

As the actor concentrated on pouring boiling water on the filtered coffee Byrd made his opening gambit.

'Tell me, Josh,' he said carefully choosing his words, 'how committed an actress was Sally Siddons?'

'Funny you should ask that because I've given it a lot of thought. During her first season here she was totally committed. Acting was her life but the same couldn't be said for the second season.'

'What was different?'

'The first reading for *Romeo* was wonderful. Viv was at his best and everyone was enthusiastic, but within days of getting on the floor there was an almost imperceptible change in Sally, something I couldn't put my finger on. She was on her own . . . solitary . . . no longer a member of the company. Even her delivery was different, the words, the meaning, the nuances were all there, but it was played from without not within until, of course, the opening performance when we saw the real Juliet. Four days later she vanished.'

Josh was close to tears, the last thing Byrd needed. Keep it low key, he told himself.

'What was she like off stage?'

'A lovely girl with no side. Quite religious, you know, when she first arrived. Mass every Sunday, but that all changed when Nigel moved in with her. Sally was God's gift for the part of Juliet. She understood the deeply religious Italians of the sixteenth century, the family vendettas and their attitude to marriage. She even took a holiday in Verona to get the feel of the place. You should have heard her at the first reading, in fact, you still can if you'd care to?'

'You mean you have a tape?'

Josh nodded.

'Wonderful,' breathed Byrd.

'If you want to hear Sally at her best I'll run it through to the final scene with Friar Laurence.'

Her voice caressed the words in a childlike way, innocent, unsullied, but Josh shivered when she said,

> 'If in thy wisdom thou canst give no help,
> Do thou but call my resolution wise,
> And with this knife I'll help it presently.'

Byrd turned it off.

'Do you,' he asked quietly, 'really believe she's committed suicide?'

'I don't know what to believe, but it's a play which always affects actors deeply. Ben had noticed the change

74

in her, kept on and on about it, but he thought she was worried about not attending confession.'

'You mean she was a lapsed Catholic?'

'Yes. I've wondered again and again whether the scene she played with Friar Laurence caused her to think of her lapse as an unforgivable sin.'

'Not these days, surely? Any twentieth century priest would understand, so too would her parents.'

'I'm not so sure about that. You need to talk to Nigel about Sir George Brown.'

'Sir George?' Byrd didn't believe what he was hearing.

'Yes. Sally's father.'

'A knight! What was he knighted for?'

'Some sort of Papal accolade, I believe, but Nigel should know. He met her parents, took quite a liking to the old man who he, laughingly, called the greenkeeper.'

Damnation, thought Byrd. Could have asked him myself. I even had the letter in my hand. He'd guessed Sally was a Catholic . . . the rosary in her small jewel box, the icon on the stairs, and a print of Raphael's *Madonna and Goldfinch* on her bedroom wall said it all. He had to see Nigel. There was just enough time to get back to the Ashcroft Room and catch the last hour of rehearsal. Nigel could fill a lot of the gaps.

He certainly made his entrance. As he stepped into the room, one of his crutches slipped to the floor and in effort to catch it the other one fell with an even greater clatter. Viv hit the table forcibly.

'That's all we need. We were so near, so nearly there.'

Janet ran towards the door, picked up both crutches and handed them to the consultant with a smile. Lorraine hadn't moved. She couldn't believe that anyone could be so crass as to burst in on an intimate rehearsal.

'Sorry about this,' said the policeman as he sat down.

Viv glared at Lorraine.

'We'll start again from the top.'

Nigel, in his role as Ferdinand, picked up a log lying in the centre of the acting area and walked into the wings which were clearly marked out in black tape. He again made his entrance carrying the log and as he was finishing his opening speech Miranda appeared looking totally relaxed. She gently placed her hand on his arm when she said the lines.

'My father is hard at study; pray now rest yourself;
He's safe for these three hours.'

Lorraine, standing half hidden behind a chair which represented a tree, spoke Prospero's lines in a curious way.

'Poor worm thou art infected!
This visitation shows it.'

Miranda tried to wrest the log from Ferdinand's arms.

'If you'll sit down
I'll bear your logs the while.'

Byrd sighed. It was a love scene beautifully played with no sign of the tenseness he'd noticed at the previous rehearsal. Even Viv would have to agree that Janet had come to terms with the part, and was revelling in it. Act III, Scene I came to an end with Viv in an exultant mood.

'We've cracked it folks, play it simply, no more embellishments. It works.'

The Superintendent's hopes for a chat with Nigel were thwarted by Lorraine who whisked the actor off to the wardrobe for his final costume fitting.

Janet picked up her script and shoulder bag, hovered for a few seconds, and then came and sat beside Byrd.

'How's your leg?'

'An aggravation, but not painful.'

'It was both aggravating and painful for us,' said Viv feelingly.

'It didn't make any difference, Mr Byrd,' said Janet softly. 'We've got it together, now.'

He knew she was aching to say something but didn't know how to begin.

'Viv, perhaps we should discuss front of house costs tomorrow?'

The director, quick on the uptake, got the message.

'FOH matters are Gerald's domain,' he said as he made for the door, 'but I'd certainly like to listen in.'

Byrd who had already mastered hopping around on one foot made much of getting to his feet. It had the desired effect.

'I'm going to take the air in the Theatre Gardens, Janet, perhaps you'd like to keep me company, make sure I don't drop these damn things again?'

'Of course. We'll go down in the lift, but won't Mrs Mayhew want to know where you are?'

So that was it. She wanted to see Georgina. Perhaps to give her the note?

'Mrs Mayhew's in Liverpool on business.' Her face fell. 'But she'll be back here in the morning.'

That seemed to satisfy her.

They weren't alone in the gardens. The lighting and sound technicians were also there sunning themselves and swilling down cans of coke.

'Lenny's a most devoted chap, never seems to leave the place.' said Byrd, testing the water.

'He does, you know, he spends a lot of time in Warwick. Mind you it's only ten minutes away.'

'But I thought he lived in Edgbaston?'

'That's where his wife and kids live.'

'You mean?'

'I can't say for sure.' She was cagey. 'It's only hear-say.'

Something else, thought Byrd, for Mayhew to follow up.

'And Alan Hunt, is he married?'

'Alan! You must be joking. He's no time for women, only horses and they continually let him down!'

Byrd laughed.

'You mean they throw him?'

'No. Only as far as his next wager.'

'He's a betting man is he . . . that must be a costly exercise.'

'Oh, he wins some times. Ups and downs, you know. But he's always good for a laugh. Says his luck will change.'

Janet sat happily for the next half hour discussing *The Tempest* which she saw simply as a romantic drama, whereas Viv looked upon it as a deeply philosophical work with romantic overtones.

'Whichever way you look at it Viv has made it work, that's all that matters.'

Byrd felt marginally better tempered as he drove back to Bletchingdon. He had a theory about Lenny in which extramarital relations didn't figure. The young man was too astute by half. He'd sussed out Mayhew, guessed she was a police officer which meant he'd been on to him too from the outset.

His fall from grace into the hellish black hole could easily have been engineered by Lenny who from all accounts was in the lighting box at the time. Didn't take much planning. While Alan had shown him up to the wardrobe the electrician could have nipped down in a matter of seconds, operated the stage trap and then waited at the bottom of the three flights of stairs for him to leave the wardrobe. Common sense would have told Lenny that he'd return to Gerald's office. All he had to do was extinguish the working light from the prompt corner and wait for him to fall into the pit before dashing back to the lighting box.

Immediately he heard the crash he would have restored the lights. No, that didn't make sense. Not quite. A second person had to be involved, someone had been upstage switching a torch off and on, and after his fall had raised the trap, before lifting a heavy 26 lb. stage weight and placing it alongside his inert body, hoping he was a goner.

By the time he took the Bletchingdon turn off the M40 he was convinced that two people were involved. Making a mental effort to thrust it to the back of his mind he was determined to enjoy a quiet evening at home with the two people who really mattered.

Kate in her final term at Middle School would be stuck into her homework. Stephanie would be in the last throes of preparing a meal, and the night was warm enough to enjoy an aperitif outside. He sighed thinking it a pity he couldn't do this more often and arrive home at a civilised hour.

He parked directly outside the front door and eased himself out of the boneshaker which he'd once derided. The windows facing the road were closed, but Stephie often forgot to open them when she arrived back from Oxford. He let himself in and slammed the door. No rushing of feet down the stairs; no voice shouting she'd nearly finished her homework. No welcoming call from the kitchen; no pungent smell of dinner cooking. Damn! Damn! Damn! It was Thursday. Kate was at the youth club while Stephanie sat around with the mums gassing over a cup of tea putting the world to rights. He poured himself a large whisky, added a modicum of ginger ale and sank back in an easy chair. Five minutes later he'd dropped off which is how his wife and daughter found him when they returned at 7.30 p.m.

'Why on earth didn't you let me know you were coming home early?'

'Because I expected you to be here.'

'But it's Thursday.'

'I know,' he said still disgruntled as the phone beside him rang.

'Yes!' he barked.

'James?' A strong Scottish accent ornamented Georgina's wonderfully throaty voice.

'Are you sitting comfortably?'

'Yes.'

'Then I'll begin! Get a load of this. Ben who's working in Liverpool with the Royal has never been abroad, and what's more he's provided an interesting slant on Sally.'

'Where are you, Georgina?'

'Hilton Park Service Station.'

'Then I'll expect you here by nine.'

'OK, and I have eaten.'

Stephanie was furious.

'You're off duty.'

'Don't let's waste time with recriminations. I'm starving.'

Kate took stock of the situation, decided to have a cup of hot chocolate and a bun and go to bed. She hated it when her father was in one of his moods, and it was even worse when they were both umpty.

By the time Georgina arrived the atmosphere in the cottage at Bletchingdon had cooled, but Stephanie kept her distance and watered the flagging hydrangeas.

Mayhew gave her boss a total run-down on the meeting at Thornton Hough making it plain that Ben had not been totally forthcoming.

'There's something going on, sir. I'm sure he knows and won't face it, and he used such a curious expression about Sally, said she was lost and lapsed.'

'She is. She's a lapsed Catholic and the daughter of a knight who's a head greenkeeper. Make sense of that. Tomorrow I'll be at Cedar Road School, interviewing Lady Brown.'

'What!'

'I'll find out why her husband was honoured. Don't ask me any questions until I've spoken to her.'

'No, sir.'

'Keep an eye on Lenny and follow him wherever he goes.'

'Yes, sir.'

'And don't humour me.'

'No, sir.'

'All right, Sergeant, I'm like a bear with a sore head.'

She smiled to herself, not a sore head, a sore leg, but let it pass.

'Incidentally, sir, the working light can only be operated from the prompt corner.'

'Interesting, that's food for thought.'

Janet Shaw was just dropping off when she heard someone knocking. It took her some seconds to realise it was her own front door that was being assaulted. She put her head

80

under the bedclothes, but the caller was insistent. She sat up shivering as she tried to make up her mind what to do. Making no move to switch on the light she slipped out of bed, and crept towards the window. Slowly, oh so slowly, she eased open the curtains until she could clearly see a figure floodlit by the street lamp. She stood motionless for a moment thinking what Mayhew had said . . . thinking she could now cope with the problem.

Only then did she relax, poke her head out of the window, and gaze down upon her unexpected visitor.

'Hi there! I'll be down in a minute.'

Chapter 4

Come, thick night,
And pall me in the dunnest smoke of hell,
That my keen knife see not the wound it makes.

Mrs Brown arrived at Cedar Road School to find Detective Superintendent Byrd in the headmistress's study discussing the latest unpopular changes in the curriculum. Miss Fairburn with only one more year to go was looking forward to getting out of education which had become a political football kicked by both teams from end to end with neither side capable of scoring goals. She'd invested in a small apartment in Gozo, with a grand view of the sea, where she could indulge her passion for archaeology until she turned up her toes.

She'd taught young Sally Brown, a bright child who started two weeks before her fifth birthday. Sally like all children prattled on about her mother which is how she learnt Mrs Brown was taking evening classes in shorthand and typing. She cajoled her into taking on the job of school secretary, and persuaded her to stay on after Sally had left to take up a scholarship at the convent.   .

Miss Fairburn told Byrd practically all he needed to know about the Brown family. Sir George, it seems, had been honoured by Pope John Paul for his valued and lifelong service to the Catholic Church. He'd become a Papal Knight, a member of the Order of St Gregory the Great. He could attend functions, so the headmistress had informed Byrd, in a magnificent dark green tailcoat and trousers trimmed with silver embroidery. To complete the picture he would have donned a cocked hat, and carried a dress sword, but the head greenkeeper eschewed such pomp and expense. He preferred to be know as plain

George to members of the golf club, despite the fact that the Queen had granted him the right to use the appellation Sir when dealing with church matters.

'It's an exclusively male preserve,' said Mrs Fairburn scathingly, 'There's no comparable honour for women, and I find it bizarre that Sally's parents could be introduced as Sir George and Mrs Brown!'

They heard the outer office door open and close.

'Megan's here. Have a heart to heart, Superintendent, while I take assembly.'

Byrd realised what a strength Miss Fairburn must have been to the Browns when their daughter vanished. He'd only one question for Mrs Brown, but would she answer it?

She was shaken when she saw the policeman sitting in the Head's study, but quickly recovered her composure when she realised bad news would have reached them at home. She liked the man, she trusted him, and above all she felt the warmth of his unspoken sympathy. When he asked her whether she knew her daughter had lapsed she answered with an honesty and directness he'd rarely encountered.

'We firmly believe, Mr Byrd, that if Sally had not lapsed she'd be with us today. As a young thing she was most impressionable, anyone could feed her outlandish information which she'd readily believe but while she was at home it was easy to keep her mind on Christian virtues. She wasn't led astray by all this mumbo-jumbo the young are being fed. At RADA she met students who were into transcendental meditation, and who talked blithely about their gurus, but their philosophy left her untouched. For most of them, I guess, it was a passing phase, but thankfully we were able to persuade Sally to take an objective view.'

She sat quietly for a moment praying that this man would find Sally.

'Do you have children, Mr Byrd?'

'Yes. One daughter, eleven years old.'

'Enjoy her innocence, it doesn't last long enough.'

Not nearly long enough, he thought, remembering how

little he'd seen of Kate as a young child. He was out on the job before she was up, and by the time he arrived home she was in bed asleep. Stephie had insisted on a strict routine, their daughter had to be secure, recognise parameters even if her father couldn't. How would he behave if Kate had vanished into thin air leaving an oddly worded note? He'd not have the Browns' faith to sustain him, and he'd jump to the only conclusion. Get back on track, he told himself. Concentrate on Sally, not Kate.

'And what, Mrs Brown, did you think of Nigel Fisher?'

'He's a nice lad, I've nothing against him, but once they were living together she stopped going to Mass. Silly really because priests understand these things, they're broad-minded. She'd have had plenty of help from Father Maloney, but she refused to see him.'

There, thought Byrd, lay the problem. What had filled the vacuum? Intuitively, he knew, that everything stemmed from her apparent loss of faith, but what had actually precipitated her disappearance?

Mrs Brown looked him straight in the eyes, and spoke as though she could read his thoughts.

'She's alive, Mr Byrd, of that I'm sure.'

Mayhew, who wanted a quick word with Janet, stood in the Ashcroft Room waiting for the actors to assemble before she bombarded Lenny with a barrage of questions. She looked down at the river below shrouded in swirling mist through which she caught glimpses of fishermen, swans and ducks, but it was the strident cries of the geese which overrode any other sound.

Josh, who arrived first, came over to have a word and enquire about the health of her boss. He seemed quite relieved to know that Dickybird was OK and would be in later that day. She wanted to talk to Nigel, but it had to look like a chance meeting, she'd try her luck at lunch time.

Lorraine and Viv arrived together. He was in a good mood and waved his hands in greeting as though dispensing a blessing.

The actors were all set to begin.

'Act II from the top,' yelled Lorraine.

Several men moved into position.

'Remember,' said Viv, 'that we plunge straight into an ongoing conversation, so lift it Gonzalo with your first line.'

The actor nodded.

> 'Beseech you, sir, be merry: you have cause,
> So have we all, of joy;'

No joy, thought Mayhew, for Sally's parents, but where were Janet and Nigel? She crept over to Josh and whispered in his ear. He smiled and shook his head.

'She's not called for this morning. You might find her in the wardrobe having her final costume fitting.'

His whisper, like that of any good actor, filled the room causing Lorraine to turn and stare balefully at him while at the same time managing to ignore his companion.

Georgina quietly left the room and made her way to the wardrobe. Helen was working her own particular magic on a blue silk dress shot through with lilac which was draped on a model.

'That's wonderful, Helen. I don't know how you do it.'

The Wardrobe Mistress, whose mouth was full of pins, beamed her appreciation.

'It's for Miranda, is it?'

Helen nodded. Mary, who'd been stuffing the washing machines with soiled clothes from the previous night's performance, giggled to herself.

'Helen's never swallowed a pin, but there's always a first time.'

Automatically Mayhew was drawn to the window. She looked down at 33 Waterside where there was no sign of life, and the curtains still drawn. She then glanced at the gems on the window still, and picked up a clear quartz crystal and held it in her left hand.

'That won't do you any good,' said Mary. 'Too many people have handled it. It needs to be cleansed. Put it under the tap, running water helps, but a warm sunny day's not the best time.'

'Should be charged when there's a full moon,' said Georgina firmly.

'Ah, you know about these things!'

'A little,' she said as she picked up a black stone.

'What's this one, and what does it do?'

'It's hematite, gives you courage, inspires you, and develops personal magnetism, though I don't think you need that.'

She winked at Georgina before filling the washing machines with soap powder, and turning them all on. The noise put paid to intimate conversation.

'There, how's that?' asked Helen as she fixed the final pin.

'It's brilliant,' said the policewoman who'd never made a dress in her life. 'When's Janet having her fitting?'

'She should be here.'

'Not if she went to bed clutching her jade crystal,' said Mary. 'It'll calm her down make her sleep for ages.'

'Don't be so daft,' said Helen abruptly. 'You take this crystal business too seriously.'

'What you need, Helen, is rose quartz, it would improve your sex life.'

'Would it now?'

Georgina thought about the selection of crystals in Janet's sitting-room. Would jade have helped her sleep, or was it merely auto-suggestion?

'Are you looking for Janet?' asked Mary.

'No.' She had to think quickly. 'I came to ask Helen a boring question.'

'Go ahead, then,' said the Wardrobe Mistress who was feeling at peace with the world because she'd just heard her son had been granted a place at Leicester University to read history.

'Have you any idea how often you need to replace the washing machines?'

'The auditor was quite pleased last year. They've been written down and owe us nothing. Roughly they have a life of five or six years, and that's using them every day of the week during the season, but the tumble drier isn't so good tempered. Lenny's had a look at it. He seems to

think we're getting unexpected surges of current because
every so often the trip goes.'

'Interesting. I think I'll have a word with him now.'

'That should explain her visit, thought Georgina, as she
ran down the stairs.

Helen stood ruminating for a few minutes.

'What did she really want, Mary?'

'God knows.'

Janet Shaw who'd had a sleepless night rose at her usual
time and made a cup of tea which she drank while listening
to the *Today* programme. She'd hardly the energy to clear
away the array of dirty cups and glasses which the two
of them had used as they'd talked the hours away. The
crystals too needed cleansing but they'd have to wait until
the 20th when the moon was full.

Despite her fatigue she recalled everything that had
been said . . . strangely it hadn't gone so deep, not this
time . . . not since she'd met Mrs Mayhew. She was
groping for a truth she couldn't unearth. Mrs Mayhew
would have helped, she'd have relaxed her, given her a
positive attitude.

There was an idea, a thin infinitesimal strand somewhere at the back of her mind. She talked out loud, not to
herself but to her sister who was killed in the coach crash.
It was her way of coping. 'The crystals aren't working,
Tess, they're draining me, giving me nothing but negative
feelings and ideas. Of course I can play the part . . . Viv
would have said . . . wouldn't he . . . wouldn't he? But
what did he mean by saying I needed a rest? Was that his
way of telling me to give up acting? But, Tess, what will
I do . . . I have nothing else . . .'

In her agony she sat in the easy chair grasping at the
cushions beneath her. 'This place is getting to me . . . I
feel Sally around . . . she's still here . . . but why did she
ever write that note telling me where to find the crystals?
And why did she hide it . . . why hide it . . . I might never
have discovered it . . .'

From somewhere in her subconscious came a blinding
truth. 'Oh God, is that what it's all about?' She slipped

her hand down the side of the seat. 'I didn't find the note, Tess, it was delivered to me. That's what they wanted, they wanted me confined, bound in by saucy doubts and fears. They're playing an evil game with me. That's what happened to Sally, isn't it? Tess, tell me that's what happened.'

Janet wept not for herself, she was now free, but for Sally who'd let them get to her. But why? That's what she'd never know.

She picked up the crystals and threw the lot into the bin before going upstairs to have a bath, to cleanse herself, knowing the sun was shining and she'd never again worry about the moon's phases.

After her frugal breakfast she found Sally's note hidden in *Great Expectations* and stuffed it in her handbag. She decided to spend half an hour before her costume fitting, in the Theatre Gardens, browse through her script and enjoy her new found freedom.

As Sergeant Mayhew went through the pass door to front of house she saw Lenny leaving by the stage door. 'Follow him,' that's what Dickybird had said. She rushed out of the building. There he was walking slowly towards his car, an A registration Escort. She swiftly skirted the side of the building and climbed into her nondescript black Metro which needed cleaning. She found a woolly cap in the glove department, crammed her long hair into it, and put on dark glasses. Moving slowly towards the car park exit she waited until she saw him drive by, then she followed close on his tail in case she lost him at the junction at the end of the bridge.

He took the A46 and drove at a steady pace to Warwick. By the time they reached the town there were two cars and a lorry between them. They turned left at the traffic lights and she nearly lost him as he took another sharp left. The two cars and the lorry continued down Jury Street leaving her directly behind his Escort in a narrow lane feeling too visible for comfort. He slowed down, took another left turn, and ended up in Warwick Castle car park which was the last thing she'd expected. He parked near the kiosk and she at the opposite end. Damn! Her bright green blouse was a giveaway. All she had with her was an old raincoat, which she kept in the boot in case she ever needed to change a tyre, and a battered straw hat. They'd have to do. At least he'd never look at her twice. She wasted a few seconds buying an illustrated guide to aid her image as a tourist.

Had Byrd and Mayhew not been concentrating on their own particular problems they might have seen each other as they passed on the A46.

Byrd's journey from Northampton to Stratford gave him a chance to nip off the main road, and into the village of Snitterfield where, as a sixteen year old, he had hoped to trace Shakespeare's antecedents.

He parked opposite the Parish Church of St James the Great, and clambered out of the car. The church was open, and on the right hand wall inside the porch he found the references he'd remembered seeing in his youth. William's grandfather, Richard, had arrived in Snitterfield in 1529, and remained a parishioner until his death in 1560 or 1561. His son John was baptised in the existing font and worshipped there until his departure for Stratford in 1552 to set up his glover's shop in Henley Street, and William's Uncle Henry farmed in Snitterfield all his life. Here, thought Byrd, ideas for the Bard's rural scenes were born. Then he read words which made his heart leap. *Manor and church records also refer to a Thomas Shaxper who may have been another uncle.* That gem wasn't there when he was working on his essay for old Hedley. If only he had time to stay in the area and research in depth, and find what no scholar had ever been able to dig up.

He wandered slowly into a lived-in church where a lot of love had been expended on cleaning every corner. The whole place reflected devotion, and the thirteenth-century chancel, improved in the nineteenth century was light and airy with beautiful mid-Victorian stained glass windows.

However, he had little time for the past, back to the treadmill to work on a highly unsatisfactory case with little hope of finding Sally Siddons. He sat for a long time in

the front pew recalling Mrs Brown's words. *She's alive,
of that I'm sure.* So many of his cases had been solved
not by a logical approach but by intuition, a sixth sense
which had led him willy-nilly in the right direction. He
knew he couldn't disregard a mother's deep seated belief.
A mother who kept her daughter's bed aired, who dusted
daily, whose belief in prayer kept her sane. A mother
who, like dozens of women throughout the land, treated
the bedroom of her missing daughter like a shrine.

While Byrd was cogitating Mayhew was following hard on
the heels of the theatre's electrician. She was amazed to
see a large queue of some two hundred visitors waiting
patiently inside the castle grounds to view the State
Rooms. Lenny had no such objective in view. Skirting
the lawn he made his way through an arch towards the
parkland outside the perimeter of the inner curtain wall.
Mayhew followed as closely as she dared, only to discover
after she'd passed through the arch that she'd lost him. For
some seconds she stood beneath a vast oak tree, peering
in all directions until the sound of footsteps alerted her
to the fact that he was ascending a vast outcrop which
towered above the tree line. She glanced through the guide
book and identified Ethelfleda's Mound. King Alfred's
daughter had, in Saxon times, fortified Warwick against
the marauding Danes, and from the summit of the mound
had commanded her army.

Despite the fact that Lenny was taking his time he
stumped up the steps like a man with a purpose. There
was no alternative but to follow him. Emerging from the
cover of the oak tree Georgina climbed steadily counting
the steps as she went. When she reached forty-seven the
steps petered out and she found herself on a narrow
winding path going ever upwards. She paused to gaze
at the breathtaking views across a verdant countryside
towards the mist covered Cotswolds. Down below on
the far side of the slowly flowing river was a disused
boathouse from which no boats emerged, and on the
near side children whose distant voices blended with the
cry of birds, were playing round rustic picnic tables.

Movement below, but nothing from above. What was Lenny doing here? A genuine desire to escape? Maybe it was his way of relaxing, getting away from the phone and the constant pressure of the job? It was the first time she'd really thought about his work. How easy it would be to press the wrong button in the middle of a performance or for the computer to develop hiccups. Despite all the modern technology there'd never be a moment to relax, total concentration was essential especially with an experimental piece of equipment.

She wanted to rip off the damn raincoat, not the garment for a heatwave, but she'd have to stick it out.

At the very moment she'd decided that Lenny had nothing to hide she heard someone moving swiftly up the steps. She quickly removed her Pentax from its case and took random shots of the broad canvas stretching out before her. She stood well back on the narrow path forcing the approaching man to pass in front of her. A middle aged Japanese, in the prime of life, not panting from his exertions who took no notice of the shabbily dressed woman charged on upwards, and out of her vision. Georgina, taking her time, followed him up yet more steps to the summit. There in a small cul-de-sac were two iron benches. Lenny sat on one and on the other, totally ignoring the lighting man, sat the energetic Japanese visitor. They were both staring at a peacock which strutted round the small enclosure uttering raucous cries before taking shelter behind a nearby bush.

There was nowhere to go, and no going back. All she could do was make for the arch to the side and behind the benches. It was covered in an iron grill to prevent intrepid visitors from committing suicide, but she managed to take a couple of shots of starlings swooping in and out of the crenellations of the Watergate Tower.

Sergeant Mayhew, ignoring the two men, strolled towards the entrance, turned and with a sudden flash of inspiration took another picture, this time of the arch. Lenny was out of shot but she'd caught the Japanese. Neither of the the two men looked put out, and neither spoke. She then turned her attention to the view of the Cotswolds, but in the lens of her camera she was able to watch the two men. At the very moment she'd decided Lenny had nothing to hide he moved closer to his contact and whispered something she couldn't catch. His hand movements which might have been meaningful to the Japanese meant nothing to the policewoman. All the stranger did was nod and listen. On the last profound nod he reached into his pocket for a slim package which he handed over; standing up he bowed slightly, and without a glimmer of a smile turned and left. As he passed Mayhew she clicked her camera, but still managed to keep Lenny in view. Casually he opened his canvas bag, smiled to himself and dropped the package inside thinking nothing of the straw-hatted woman in the dirty raincoat with her back to him.

Georgina followed the Japanese who much to her surprise joined the queue for the State Apartments. Business and pleasure!

Mayhew taking her time, made sure she didn't reach the car park until Lenny had gone, then she chucked her old raincoat in the boot, threw her woollen cap in the air, and shouted *olé*!

As she drove back to the theatre her jubilation gradually evaporated as she thought about her mother . . . the phone call late last night . . . the desperation in the quiet voice . . . the inability to live on her own . . . waking up each day knowing there was nothing . . . no one to care for . . . what was the point?

Georgina faced the truth. In this sort of state her mother couldn't be left on her own, and there was no way she'd move south. To live among the Sassenachs would be selling her birthright. There was nothing for it, but to uproot herself from a job she loved in a place she'd come to love. The last thing in the world she wanted was a transfer, but there was no alternative. She'd never had so much freedom. Being stuck with her mother would be nearly as hellish as life with her ex. *Where are you going? When will you be back? Shall I get supper for you? Would you like haddock or cod? Do your undies want washing? Who was that man ringing you? Have you seen your father lately?*

92

She adored Edinburgh but the thought of being incarcerated with her mother left her feeling unutterably depressed. She shouldn't have leapt at the chance of working on another case with Byrd. She should have taken her leave in Scotland as planned, come clean with Sir Charles, told him the score.

Byrd sat for nearly two hours in the front pew of the church of St James the Great in Snitterfield. He was no longer interested in architecture, for his mind, often described by his colleagues as machiavellian, was considering a score of reasons why a deeply religious young woman had vanished without trace. He was frustrated, angry with himself for not coming up with a single tenable theory.

It was nearly lunch-time, he'd get back there and tackle Nigel Fisher head on. Sit on a bench in the theatre gardens, wait for the morning rehearsal to come to an end and then pounce.

Twenty minutes later he'd parked, found an empty bench, thrown his crutches to the ground and slipped off his jacket. He sat watching a group of children and their teacher finishing off a picnic lunch before making their way to the brass rubbing centre at the other end of the gardens. It was housed in what used to be part of the old vicarage adjacent to Holy Trinity. Soon after the church clock struck one he saw Josh and Lorraine with other members of the company making their way along Waterside towards the Dirty Duck. A few minutes later Lorraine dashed out of the pub, across the road and into the gardens running hell for leather towards the green-room and shouting at someone coming from the opposite direction.

'Have you found her?'

'No,' yelled Nigel Fisher as he stopped alongside the bench, 'but perhaps Mr Byrd has, that's his job, isn't it?'

'What are you saying?'

'You're lame, you're a lousy actor, and no one would ever take you for a management consultant. 'You're a policeman, it sticks out a mile, with time to sit in the sun, it seems!'

'Who's missing, Mr Fisher?' He felt sick. He knew. But he had to ask.

'Janet. She should have had her final fitting this morning. Helen was quite ratty when she didn't turn up.'

'Wasn't she at rehearsal?'

'No, because she wasn't called.'

'I know,' said Lorraine, having a sudden brainwave, 'She's with your Mrs Mayhew.'

Byrd reached for his phone, tapped out a number. 'Georgina, are you on your own.'

'Of course.'

Where are you?'

She knew instantly there was trouble ahead.

'Passing the Moat House.'

'Get back here immediately. I'm in the Theatre Gardens.' He switched off, stared at Lorraine, and shook his head.

'Where else have you looked?'

'Everywhere. I couldn't raise her on the phone so Gerald went across to 33 and opened up. I thought she might have overslept but she wasn't there.'

'Where's Viv?'

'He's tied up with the sponsors. They're lunching at Hall's Croft, but he'll be back in time for the rehearsal.'

Byrd felt angry with himself, and guilty. He'd been sitting dreaming up theories in Snitterfield when he should have been in the theatre on call.

At that moment the air was filled with the sound of children screaming.

'Little darlings,' said Nigel furiously, 'this garden isn't a playground.'

There were more screams. Byrd was on his feet.

'Come on, they're not playing games. That's fear.'

Forgetting his crutches he clutched his phone and limped at an incredible speed towards a couple of children who should have been concentrating on brass rubbing. They were standing by the river bank staring into the water. The teacher, who'd thought all her charges were in the centre, heard the screaming and came running imagining the worst.

94

Byrd hardly needed to look into the water.

'Please, Madam, take these children back to the centre, and wait there until a woman police officer arrives. She'll need to talk to you all.'

The teacher now more composed than her charges took the hands of the screaming children and led them away.

'You expected this,' said Nigel bitterly, 'so why the hell didn't you prevent it?'

The three of them looked down on the slight figure of Janet Shaw who lay with her eyes open and her hair floating like weeds around her face. It was too much for Nigel.

'She's drowned herself,' he sobbed, 'like Ophelia . . . she's like Ophelia

her garments, heavy with their drink,
Pull'd the poor wretch from her melodious lay
To muddy death.'

'Cut it out, Nigel, this is for real,' said Lorraine abruptly.

'She didn't drown,' said Byrd, 'neither was she singing when she died. She's been murdered. Look at the colour of the water. It's bloody. And by God I'm going to find the murderer.'

The sweat was pouring off him . . . he felt heady . . . only then did he realise he'd run without the aid of his crutches. *Forget the damn leg . . . concentrate . . . so many clues destroyed.* The small muddy inlet shielded by bushes and trees was covered with children's footprints, nevertheless from now on it would be kept clear, but where the hell was Mayhew?

Lorraine crept closer to take a look murmuring to herself as tears poured down her face, but the policeman whose hearing was acute heard every syllable.

Byrd pulled at Nigel's arm.

'Come away, come away both of you and stand over there. Make sure no one comes near while I make some phone calls.'

He staggered slightly, and leaned back against the tree

in an effort to relieve the pressure on his right leg. Ignoring police procedure he rang his Chief Constable direct. Sir Charles listened, said he'd set everything in motion, and ordered Detective Superintendent Byrd to stay put.

Mayhew who'd had difficult in parking saw Lorraine who, ignoring Byrd's orders to remain *in situ*, had rushed over to the bench to pick up the crutches and jacket.

'Lorraine,' she yelled, 'where is he? What's happened?'

'He's down by the water,' cried the stage manager, who kept running with Mayhew hard on her heels.

She saw Nigel staring in her direction, his expression anything but friendly, then she saw her boss leaning against the willow tree. Her joy at finding him unhurt was immediately dispelled when she caught sight of Janet's body. Pain and anger shooting through her body brought her to a standstill. *Why . . . why . . . why . . . ? It didn't make sense . . . this lovely girl who had been frightened, but who eventually seemed able to cope with the fear, real or imaginary, was dead. A mindless senseless killing.*

Janet's face in repose was beautiful . . . she hadn't expected to die . . . she'd known her killer.

Byrd looked at his sergeant bleakly as he automatically slipped on his jacket.

'Sergeant, the body was found by two youngsters who are in the brass rubbing centre with their teacher. Have a brief word with them, and see if any of the other kids noticed anything. I'll stay put until the pathologist and forensic arrive. Mr Fisher and Lorraine can leave, and Lorraine make sure the company keeps clear of this area. We don't need another army of footsteps.'

'Hadn't I better ring Viv? He's lunching at Hall's Croft. He'll need a replacement as soon as possible and an understudy for this afternoon's rehearsal?'

He was staggered.

'You mean he'll rehearse?'

'Of course. We open to the Press in six days. I'd better alert the assistant director, but on second thoughts I think I'll read in Miranda's part this afternoon, give him time to sort himself out.'

Byrd shook his head as she made her way back to the theatre.

Viv was feeling satisfied both with the sponsor's largesse and the grilled plaice which was browned exactly to his taste. He was sitting where he most liked to sit, facing the portrait of Wriothesley, Earl of Southampton Shakespeare's earliest benefactor. There was ample time to take their coffee in the garden. A blissful haven of peace. He was annoyed at being called to the phone, especially by Lorraine who should know better.

'Can't it wait?' he growled.

There was a long pause.

'Viv, I don't know how to tell you this.'

Another long pause. He waited uneasily.

'What is it Lorraine?' softly this time.

'It's Janet . . .'

'She's not ill . . . is she?'

A thin smile crept over Lorraine's face. At least she'd got his attention.

'Less than an hour ago she was found . . . drowned . . .'

'What!'

'Well not exactly drowned, she's floating in the reeds.'

'Why did she do it, for Christ's sake!'

'She didn't. She's been murdered.'

'Murdered! Janet!'

He stood with his eyes closed hanging on to the phone. He was shaking, unable to speak, but his mind was full to bursting . . . he'd known . . . he'd known all along . . . there was something indescribably foul at work . . . he should have brought Byrd in sooner . . . now he needed another Miranda . . . even worse than last time when Sally had actually played the opening . . . he needed a first class rocklike Miranda who could support Josh . . . yes . . . he needed to cosset Josh, Josh who would be all to pieces.

'Dan could take this afternoon's rehearsal, Viv, and I'll read in Miranda while you pull out all the stops.'

'God, what a strength you are, Lorraine.' He still hung on to the phone.

'Who do you suggest?'

'Anita Jennings?'

'Too old.'

'Angie Peters.'

'She'd look right . . . voice isn't too mature. Not a bad idea. It's *The Shrew* tonight at the Barbican. She's playing Bianca. I'll see if I can get someone to take over from her immediately.' Then he remembered. 'Where's Janet now?'

'Still in the water by the river bank.'

'What! Why the hell don't they move her?'

'Something to do with despoiling the evidence.'

'For God's sake! I'll get down there straight away.'

He slammed down the phone. Meanwhile Lorraine wished she could be a fly on the wall at the meeting of the Titans, but she'd not have a chance, there was a traumatic rehearsal to get through.

Fortunately, Mr Wainwright, the Birmingham-based pathologist who lived in Warwick was at home preparing a lecture when he received an urgent call from, Fraser Drummond, the Chief Constable of Warwickshire.

Drummond and Sir Charles Suckling had lost no time in setting up a *modus operandi*. Warwickshire, one of the smallest forces in the country, was stretched to its limits having been hit by a flu bug which attacked HQ. Drummond admitted to Sir Charles that he was damn glad that the 1968 amalgamation had produced regional crime squads all ready to help each other, and that Byrd was on the spot. He was to be left in charge of the case with Sergeant Mayhew as his right hand (or right leg depending how one looked at it) with all other facilities being provided locally.

Wainwright who arrived slightly ahead of the forensic officers found a Detective Superintendent he'd never met sitting on the grass.

'Afternoon, Mr Byrd. Murder have we? No sexual connotations, I guess, not in this spot at this time of day. My God, she was a pretty lass.'

'It's history repeating itself,' said the policeman softly.

'Everything about this case seems to be connected with the Bard.'

'In what way?'

'In 1580, when Shakespeare was only sixteen, a girl named Katherine Hamlett was drowned in this river, possibly at this spot, under the branches of a great willow. It was a *cause célèbre,* and the inquest dragged on for nearly eight weeks.'

'And the outcome?'

'Accidental death, but my guess is that it was suicide, and Shakespeare, knowing that, drew on it when depicting Ophelia's death.'

'You go too deep, my friend.'

'Or not deep enough!'

Shortly afterwards eight officers, based in Stratford, arrived to rope off the area and close the gardens.

While they were at work the schoolteacher and children from St Mary's in Banbury were making their way to Holy Trinity before returning home. Mayhew had been quite impressed by the recall of the two youngsters who'd long since stopped crying. They were now the centre of attention and enjoying it. Each time they told the story Janet's hair was longer, her eyes bluer and the water bloodier.

Viv arrived at the scene of the crime shortly after the pathologist and insisted on being allowed through the cordon to speak to the superintendent. Byrd was quietly authoritative, keeping Viv well away from the muddy bank, as his men carefully lifted the body out of the water and laid it gently on a stretcher. Before the ambulance men left the site Mr Wainwright made a preliminary examination.

'It was very quick, Mr Byrd.' He lifted up her T-shirt and pointed to a vicious gash between her shoulder blades. 'It's a downward stroke, straight through the heart. Her killer would have been covered in blood. You're looking for a largish dagger, Superintendent. This was murder with intent, I'd hazard, not a mugger otherwise he'd have taken her bag.'

'You're damn right,' said Byrd who'd glanced at the

contents of her sodden handbag, and found more than he'd dare hope for. Money, cheque cards, make-up and the elusive note which, according to Janet, had been written by Sally Siddons.

Viv, who'd remained silent, wanted to vomit. He'd seen plenty of simulated deaths in *Macbeth*, *Hamlet* and *Caesar* but never, despite his forty-four years, a real corpse.

'You OK, Viv?' asked Byrd.

'I feel sick. Why pick on two actresses who've never hurt anyone, and what's he done with Sally's body?'

'We don't know whether Sally was killed, and Janet may not have been murdered by a man.'

'You mean a woman could have done this?'

'Easily,' said Wainwright. 'She's only a slip of a thing, and she was surprised. Knifed in the back with no time to fight back.'

'How long has she been dead?' asked Byrd.

'Allowing for water and air temperature, I'd say she died between ten and eleven this morning.'

'Where were you at the time, Sergeant?'

'Following one of your hunches, sir.'

'I see.' He didn't, but the matter could wait. 'Did you rehearse this morning, Viv?'

'Yes.'

'Everyone present except Janet?'

'Yes.'

'Sergeant, interview the wardrobe staff and technicians, find out where they were between ten and eleven.'

At least I know where one of the technicians was, thought Georgina.

Gerald came running across the grass. Viv looked at him in surprise. He'd never seen his laid-back colleague out of breath. Now what was up?

'Superintendent, I've just had a word with your wife.'

'My wife!' That was the last thing he needed.

'She said to let you know she had a slight skirmish with a lorry as she drove into Oxford this morning.'

'What!'

'She's all right. She's had a check up at the Radcliffe and apart from bruised ribs she's OK.'

Byrd was stunned. Speechless.

'She apologised for calling you, but said she's stuck at a garage in Oxford waiting to hear whether the car is a write-off. She thought you'd be uptight . . . it being new.'

'I couldn't care less about the car.'

Now what did he do? It would take him an hour to reach Oxford, make sure she was OK and an hour back. Two hours out at the most important moment in a case. He took a deep breath. There was no alternative. Stephie was alive . . . Janet dead . . . he was there to find a killer.

'Call her back, will you Gerald. She'll be suffering from shock. Tell her to get a taxi home, like now, and forget the damned car. Tell her I'll be back just as soon as I can.'

No one spoke. The two officers from forensic and Wainwright exchanged glances, and Mayhew chewed her bottom lip causing it to bleed. She had to stand by while he attempted to thrust the knowledge, that his wife too could have died, to the back of his mind. She could stand it no longer.

'Sir, let me hold the fort. Not much more can be done today.'

'It's not on, Sergeant, the show must go on . . . isn't that what they say? Gerald,' he yelled after the departing figure.

The manager rushed back expecting another message for Stephanie, but the policeman surprised him.

'We need space, something bigger than John's office to serve as the scene-of-crime office. If you can't accommodate us then I'll bring in a mobile.'

Gerald couldn't believe his ears. He'd expected Byrd to have a change of mind, to leave the case in Georgina's hands and get over to Oxford immediately. Even a more loving message would have been some help to his wretched wife, but all he was concerned with was office space. Viv and James Byrd had a lot in common. Nothing, absolutely nothing, must be allowed to get in the way of a production. He shook his head.

'We've nothing, absolutely nothing in the theatre, but . . .'

'Yes?'

'How about 33, Waterside, now that Janet's . . . it's small but . . .'

'An excellent suggestion. It'll suit us very well.'

'I'll get someone in to tidy up. There was quite a party last night, glasses and cups all over the shop.'

'No,' said Mayhew quickly. 'Forensic must get in there, do a check, collect all the debris, and then we'll move in. I'll arrange, sir, for a computer and fax to be installed before the day's out.'

Byrd just nodded, wondering whether the seat belt had caused Stephie's bruises, and whether anyone had witnessed the accident?

Troubles never come singly, thought Wainwright as he made his final notes.

'OK, you chaps, take the lady away and I'll attend her in the mortuary later this afternoon.'

The police did a thorough job in the gardens combing the place looking for clues, but no sign of a dagger or large knife. At 2.30 p.m. frogmen arrived to search the river bed, but all they managed to turn up were empty wine and beer bottles, and an antiquated food mixer jettisoned by an untidy holiday-maker from a hired narrow boat.

Much to Lorraine's annoyance Mayhew interrupted the lack lustre rehearsal to check that everyone in the cast had been present at the morning rehearsal. There was no heart in any of the actors, they sat miserably, or acted miserably despite the fact that the assistant director and stage manager were bent on getting a performance from them. Much better to have cancelled the whole thing, thought Georgina, but that's not how theatre works. Josh seemed to have retreated into a world of his own, but the aura round Nigel was unmistakably hostile. He directed venomous glances in her direction while at the same time repeating his lines parrot fashion to Lorraine who was standing in for Miranda. The policewoman was impressed by the stage manager's ability to hold the company together. She wondered whether Viv could have coped as well.

The artistic director was halfway to London, intent

on seeing John Butler and two actresses, both possible replacements for Janet. One playing Bianca, and the other understudying the part of the Shrew. Both were dependable but Angie would be better able to cope with Josh who was a highly nervous and unpredictable actor. He shouldn't have left him to Lorraine's far from tender mercies . . . they just didn't hit it off. Why hadn't he cancelled the rehearsal . . . taken Josh with him . . . let him talk to Angie . . . start off on the right foot? There was no one more capable than Lorraine, always one step ahead, sometimes he relied on her too much, but would she have the sense to go easy with Josh? Perhaps he should have deferred the opening night, but he'd never done so before, not in twenty years as a director . . . not good for the theatre . . . or was he worrying about his own image?

Mayhew interviewed the technicians in the circle bar. There were five, two whom she'd not seen before who had played tennis from 9.30 a.m. to 11.30 a.m., followed by a shower and coffee before returning to the theatre. Alan Hunt, who said he'd worked all morning on the sound effects for his sister's school play being performed in Tewkesbury in ten days time, had no one to confirm his statement. Then there was Johnny, Ben's replacement, who had cleaned the lens of lanterns suspended on barrels over the stage. Any number of persons passing through the wings would have seen him. A barrel, Mayhew had learnt, was a cylindrical aluminium bar. Lenny surprised her. He made no secret of taking a breather and visiting Warwick Castle. He even produced the stub of his entrance ticket.

Meanwhile Detective Superintendent Byrd was just hobbling away from the scene of the crime when a gaggle of photographers, and avid journalists descended on him. The questions came thick and fast, the cameramen clicked away taking full length shots of the injured policeman clearly featuring the crutches, and close-ups of his face which spoke volumes. Byrd, however, was succinct.

'*Janet Shaw who was playing the part of Miranda in*

The Tempest, her most important role to date with the RSC, was murdered by a person or persons unknown. Investigations are at a preliminary stage, and at this moment there is nothing more to report.'

The news was too late for the evening papers but not for the innumerable flashes on radio and TV.

Stephanie, who'd taken a taxi as instructed by the theatre manager, expected to find James at home waiting for her looking a trifle concerned, maybe, but he'd play down the emotion. He always did. He was a master of understatement, but she understood his coded messages. His absence upset her. For the first time that day she wept. Kate cuddled up to her as they sat on the sofa knowing her mother needed comforting but knowing nothing about the accident. She couldn't talk about it, she tried not to think about it, but the images wouldn't go away. At 6 o'clock Stephanie switched on the TV to get the news and found herself staring at a familiar face.

'It's Daddy. Look it's Daddy!' Kate jumped up and put her finger on the screen. 'Look!'

'Shush. Just listen.'

Stephanie relaxed. Now she knew, knew why he hadn't been waiting for her.

'She'd dead, Mummy, she's been killed. Now everyone will know Daddy's at Stratford and he made me promise not to tell.'

'Yes, darling, but you didn't did you?'

'No.'

'Good. Shall we get a special supper ready for him? He'll be tired and hungry.'

'And sad, Mummy.'

'Yes, that too.'

In an old council house in Park Avenue North, not too far from Northampton Golf Club, the Browns also sat watching the 6 o'clock news. When the newscaster announced that Janet Shaw had been found murdered

104

Megan Brown gave a sudden cry like an animal in pain before she passed out.

Her husband switched off the television, lifted his wife on to the sofa, and rang their doctor whose surgery was less than a quarter of a mile down the road.

George Brown felt dizzy thinking that he too was going to pass out. He looked down on his wife thinking the worst . . . thinking she might be dead. He knelt beside her, felt for her pulse, and breathed a sigh of relief when he realised she was still alive. 'Thank you, Lord,' he whispered as he lifted her on to the sofa and placed two cushions under her head before covering her with a blanket.

Doctor Chalmers, who'd cared for the Browns for the past eleven years, knew by the sound of George's voice that the matter was urgent. It took him five minutes to reach the house on foot, much quicker than getting the car out, and trying to park the damn thing. The doctor who had originally treated Megan with tranquillizers when Sally vanished had realised her religion was more beneficial than the tablets and had stopped prescribing them. He opened the front door and walked straight into the sitting-room.

'Take the cushions away, George, she should be horizontal.'

He felt her pulse, and as he finished with his stethoscope Megan moaned slightly and opened her eyes.

'Take it easy Mrs Brown. The best thing for you is a cup of tea. You've fainted nothing more than that.'

George was too overcome to speak, all he could do was cross himself.

Doctor Chalmers, who'd also been watching the TV news, realised what had caused his patient to black out. He knew Megan believed Sally was still alive, and steadfastly refused to accept the fact that she'd never see her daughter again. Now she'd have to come to terms with the unpalatable truth that Sally too may have been murdered. The doctor's eyes misted over. His own daughter was Sally's age. Life without her would be unimaginable.

Fraser Drummond was also watching the news. He sat

there scarcely able to believe his eyes. That damned police officer from Oxfordshire was lame, not only that he was dressed in a denim suit, and to crown it all, *no tie*. There he stood scowling at the damned camera saying nothing then, when he eventually spoke, he said it all in two terse sentences. Drat the man. The Warwickshire Force would become a joke. A murder case in the hands of the walking wounded. He picked up the phone.

In the study of an elegant manor house outside Enstone Sir Charles Suckling sat listening to the radio. Byrd sounded tired, but he was quietly firm with the interviewer. That was somewhat unusual. Then the phone beside him rang.

'Yes?'

'Drummond here. I've just seen the television news. You didn't tell me that officer of yours was crippled, neither did you tell me that he's one of those way-out fellows who doesn't dress properly.'

'He gets results, Fraser, isn't that what matters?'

'The image matters.'

'This time he's dressed for the part he was playing . . . all that will change.'

'I sincerely hope so, but he's not fit, not capable of coping with a murder.'

'If I were a betting man I'd put money on him. He's also got Sergeant Mayhew with him. She's hot stuff, about to be promoted. She'll hear the good news when things have quietened down.'

Fraser Drummond wasn't interested in the elevation of sergeants in another force. The only thing that mattered was a murder in his parish.

'Are there any leads which suggest that the murder of Janet Shaw is connected with the disappearance of Sally Siddons?'

'None so far. Siddons left a note which suggests she left of her own volition.'

'Charles, I have a couple of good men on another case. I can have them available, immediately. Both Warwickshire men with plenty of contacts.'

Sir Charles used his diplomatic skills.

106

'Fraser, why don't we get together tomorrow? Discuss the matter with Byrd? Put your mind at rest.

'Well . . .'

'I'll pick you up at eleven hundred hours.

The Major laughed, despite himself.

'You never miss a trick, Charles. Great business must be wrought ere noon.'

Chapter 5

Now boast thee, death, in thy possession lies
A lass unparalleled.

The two men from forensic, known in the force as Laurel
and Hardy, did a swift appraisal of 33 Waterside, collecting
cups, glasses, a diary, letters, notes on the recent production, scripts and a heap of coloured stones which they
salvaged from the bin. Other than that there was little
of interest in the house; the furnishings belonged to the
RSC and the few mementoes and ornaments told them
nothing. Two technicians followed them in to install a
computer, phone and Fax and by 6.30 p.m. Byrd was
sitting comfortably in the easy chair calling Stephanie while
Mayhew brewed tea. Kate answered the phone.

'Daddy,' she screamed, her voice going up an octave,
'we saw you . . . you looked very cross.'

Stephanie turned off the grill and dashed into the hall.

'Are you all right, James? It must have been a ghastly
shock. You weren't expecting it, were you?'

'If I'd been expecting it, Stephie, I might have been able
to prevent it, but don't worry about me, darling. More to
the point, how are you?'

'I'm OK now. I've been a bit weepy, but I guess that's
the shock.'

'What happened?'

'You know the roundabout where the A423 and the
A40 meet?'

'Yes.'

'My way was clear when I started but a large petrol
tanker came out of the blue at a hell of a lick catching
the back of the car and turning it over.'

He broke into a cold sweat. *A petrol tanker . . . a fireball*

. . . could all have been over . . . why couldn't he speak? At last he managed to stop shaking.

'How did you escape?'

'Climbed through the open window.'

'Thank God for the heat wave.'

'That's what the guy said who helped me out.'

'You've had a thorough check-up?'

'Yes. They were very good at the Radcliffe . . . one of their voluntary drivers wanted to drive me home, but I was concerned about the car.'

'Stephie, don't you realise the car doesn't matter a damn? And what's more you're going to take it easy for a couple of weeks. Spratt and Salisbury can manage without you. Put your feet up and do nothing, and don't wait supper for me. I'll be home by eight, then we'll talk seriously about the future.'

'We'll wait for you but we're not going to talk about the future. Bye darling.'

Mayhew heard it all, saw the beads of sweat on his forehead. She bided her time, let him calm down. Talk about the future? What was he getting at? As they sipped their tea she went through the morning's sortie in detail. Lenny's carefully planned assignation with the Japanese, the packet which changed hands, and her own attempts at photography which Laurel and Hardy had taken with them to get developed. Byrd was interested in the exact times.

'Can you be specific?'

'I think so. At about 9.20 a.m. I was standing around waiting for the actors to arrive, hoping for a quick word with Janet. Josh told me she'd not been called for the morning rehearsal because she was having her final fitting. After that I went along to the wardrobe maintenance, where they were all hard at it, not to talk to them but to take a look at 33 Waterside. The curtains were still drawn and no sign of life which led me to believe Janet was having a lie-in. At about 10.15 a.m. as I was about to check 33, I saw Lenny leaving by the stage door so I followed him and you know the rest.'

'Have you checked where the other technicians were?'

'Yes. Alan Hunt's the only one whose alibi can't be

109

confirmed. He was busy preparing a tape for a school performance.'

Byrd hummed softly to himself as he doodled before scribbling half a dozen lines.

'Well Georgina,' he said at last, 'what would be your next move?'

She wrinkled her nose as she mentally rearranged the ideas which had been flitting through her mind all afternoon.

'First I'd have a straight talk with Nigel Fisher, then I'd order Ben Adams down here, and while waiting for him to arrive I'd delve into the occult by questioning Lorraine and Mary about their astrological practices. I'm also inordinately curious to know what Lenny is up to. His extramural peccadilloes may not be related to the murder but I don't think we can ignore them. Lastly I'd check Sally's final note to Viv with the one she left for Janet.'

Byrd smiled at her, his first smile of the day, before handing her the notes he'd made.

a) Get Ben Adams down here
b) Interview Nigel Fisher
c) What do Lenny's shenanigans amount to?
d) Question the wardrobe staff about crystallomancy
e) See Sally's parents again
f) Compare Sally's 2 notes
g) Trace Janet's relatives

'You get an alpha plus, Georgina. Ring Ben Adams tonight, and let Nigel Fisher know I want him here at nine in the morning.'

'That's a bit hard, isn't it? Bringing him back here? This was his home.'

'Might jog his memory. We've no time for sentiment. Get going, Sergeant, sit and mull over the case at home, make notes, write down everything that Janet said to you. Tomorrow we'll make up our minds how we're going to divide the load.'

As Georgina drove home she realised that the last hour in Dickybird's company was worth enduring a whole day's hassle. In her own curious way she was fond of the man, knew she'd miss him if she transferred to Edinburgh, but she'd no option, her mother might go over the top, take an overdose, and if that happened she'd live with the guilt for ever.

She could hear herself screaming with delight as her father ran into the sea carrying her on his back, and then her father massaging her mother's back with suntan oil. They were happy, the three of them. Her mother vivacious and always laughing, her father happy-go-lucky until the business grew in size, then he was out more and more. Meetings in Paris, Rome, Zurich. At first he took her mother with him, until the meetings absorbed all his time, then her mother stopped going abroad. She was more lonely in Zurich with him, than in Edinburgh without him. Her daughter, not her husband, became the focus of her life. Finally she had had to face the fact that he was surrounded by attractive young women who knew their way around. That was when the marriage really ended, but for six years they'd carried on the farce, before he finally left.

As soon as Mayhew arrived home she called her mother who sounded unutterably depressed. No, she didn't want to attend the Over-60's Club. No, she didn't go to the theatre anymore. No, she didn't want to spend a week or two in Oxford. Only when her daughter said she'd be applying for a transfer did her mood change. Suddenly there was meaning to her life, something to live for.

There was no going back, thought Georgina. No going back.

Byrd opened the door, and stood there savouring the aroma of coq au vin, his favourite dish. Stephanie hearing the latch dashed into the hall, and fell into his arms. She was gloriously alive, not a mark on her face. From upstairs came the sound of *Stay* sung by Shakespeare, Kate's favourite pop duo, a perfect homecoming. Funny how he couldn't escape the Bard. They hugged and kissed each other, two people both lucky to be alive.

'Come on,' said Stephanie, 'I'll pour you a G and T.'

'I'm quite capable of acting as barman.'

'But . . . ' Only then did she realise he wasn't using his crutches.

'Where are they?'

'In the car where they're staying. I'm going to manage with a stick from now on.'

'And you dare tell me to take it easy.' She laughed, 'you'll never change, James.'

'I changed today, at least my outlook changed, but we'll talk about it after supper.'

Two hours later when Kate was tucked up in bed Stephanie listened to an idea which had been mooted in the past, but never taken seriously. James had made up his mind to resign from the force and take up a job, one which had been offered him six months previously. The Principal of an Oxford college, who ran two-month courses for businessmen, was on the lookout for mature linguists, not academics, who could deal with up-to-date idioms used in the legal profession, and terms employed in the import-export business. Two of his cases had taken him abroad, one to Germany and the other to France. On both occasions his command of the language had proved more than adequate.

Stephanie didn't feel it was the right time to think about change. Felt they were both suffering from shock, and a monumental step like resigning from the Force should only be taken when he'd solved the present case, and she was back at work.

And there the matter was left.

The following morning Georgina was back in Stratford way ahead of her boss. She found that the man left on duty at the scene of the crime, who spoke with a wonderful Welsh lilt, had had an undisturbed watch. The area near the bank was clearly sealed off by red and white striped tape, and the rest of the gardens were now open to the public.

She then let herself into 33 Waterside, took in the milk which hadn't been cancelled and was surprised to find a letter on the mat addressed to Detective Superintendent Byrd. She was about to pick it up when a sixth sense told

112

her to exercise caution. Using a clean handkerchief she placed it on the occasional table, and as she did so noticed a string of messages on the fax. She tore them off as Byrd let himself in.

'Good morning, Georgina. Are we in business?'

'We are. A letter for you on the table, not handled, and umpteen messages.'

He scanned the first sheet which was a photo-copy of Sally's note telling Janet where the crystals were buried.

'Good. We'll compare the calligraphy with Viv's note.'

He read the second sheet.

'Hell! That's all we need.'

SIR CHARLES SUCKLING AND MAJOR DRUMMOND ARRIVING AT 11.30.

The third sheet gave them cause for thought.

Fingerprints on the mugs and glasses were made by two people. One set checked with the victim's prints, and the other dabs belonged to an unknown visitor.

'Strange isn't it,' he mused, 'for two people to sit and drink the hours away . . . has all the hallmarks of a friendly encounter . . . but if the visitor was the murderer why didn't he or she carry it out *in situ* where there'd be no witnesses?'

'Possibly someone who knew X saw him enter?'

'And what did they discuss? What did Janet know?'

'She may have guessed what happened to Sally. Perhaps that's what this is all about. Perhaps she could finger him?'

James Byrd didn't agree with this hypothesis. It didn't feel right, but he couldn't argue because he could think of nothing better.

'Incidentally, Georgina, I talked with the Station Officer who's had all the bins in the area searched for the missing weapon, and blood soaked clothing. Useless. Absolutely nothing.'

'The milk wasn't cancelled, sir, maybe the roundsman remembers whether any lights were on in the early hours of the morning.'

'Milk! That means a cuppa right now, does it?'

She laughed. 'Yes if you tell me how you're going to manage without crutches.'

'Willpower and foolhardiness supported by a strong walking stick. Now let me take a look at that letter.' He held it gingerly, and slit it open with his pocket knife. The message was short. A couple of lines typed on a sheet of A4.

> To mourn a mischief that is past and gone
> Is the next way to draw new mischief on.

'What on earth does that mean?'

Mayhew leant over his shoulder and read it through twice.

'Could mean exactly what it says. A second murder if we delve too deeply.'

'A third,' he growled, 'if we assume that Sally Siddons is dead.'

'But why actresses? Is it coincidence?'

'That's what we have to find out, and quickly, before another murder occurs.' He sank back into the easy chair and closed his eyes. 'A motive, a damned motive is what we need, and fast.'

Georgina looked at his face, more strain there than she'd ever seen. He needed something stronger than a cup of tea. A double brandy would make more sense, but she dutifully filled the kettle.

He was damned certain the murderer was a member of the company . . . had to be . . . someone who knew the theatre inside out . . . who knew enough on the technical side to try and silence him by precipitating him into a black hole. Someone who was guilty . . . who'd been expecting a police enquiry . . . someone who knew exactly what had happened to Sally.

His cogitation was disturbed by Laurel and Hardy who arrived carrying a box of casts taken from footprints and a selection of clearly numbered plastic bags containing crystals, cheque cards, an address book, a letter and a post-card of Witley Court. Odd, no postmark, but the picture showed a magnificent classical palace in Worcestershire, circa 1870, but where the hell was Witley Court? The address and the message on the postcard were hardly legible having been soaked in the river.

Laurel presented him with a packet of Mayhew's latest artistic efforts which included six unidentifiable English landscapes, three of the Watergate Tower, and several of crowds waiting to see the State Rooms.

'What the hell were you doing?'

'Trying to look like a tourist' she said sharply.

'Well you succeeded admirably!'

At last he found what he was looking for.

'Ah that's better. It's a splendid camera. Everything's clearly defined.'

'Helps, sir, if the photographer knows how.'

He ignored the gibe and peered carefully at each one. Lenny sitting on a bench looking at a peacock showing off its plumage; Lenny looking into space; a foreigner, obviously Japanese, sitting on a bench with a grill covered arch behind him; the back of the Japanese striding down a narrow pathway; the Japanese joining a queue of sightseers; finally Lenny disappearing among the trees.

The letter postmarked Sidmouth and dated 10th December 1990, although wet, was legible and in reasonable condition. Byrd fingered it carefully. The printed heading told them it was from St David's Residential Home, and in a spidery uneven scrawl wished Janet a happy Christmas and hoped she'd buy herself something useful with the two pound cheque from her loving grandma.

'Not much you can buy with two pounds these days,' said Georgina.

'She's living in the past when two pounds was money,' said Byrd sadly. 'She must be Janet Shaw's only living relation, and now we have to tell an old lady the awful truth?'

'No you don't,' said Laurel, 'we've checked. She died in February during the flu epidemic.'

115

Mayhew breathed a sigh of relief. One of the worst aspects of the job was imparting bad news.

She opened the box containing the casts and spread them on the floor. All had been overprinted with impressions made by smaller feet which virtually obliterated the type of shoe but fortunately not the size.

'A man, I'd say, sir. Not many women wear size 8's.'

'You could be right.' He picked up the plastic bag containing the postcard of Witley Court and peered at the smudged address. 'At last!' he yelled. 'At last! Look at this. Do you see, Sergeant, there's no stamp. The addressee had to pay the postage and just look at that writing. I'd lay fifty to one it matches Sally's last note to Viv.'

'I'm not taking you on,' grinned Georgina.

In a few seconds he'd recovered, his eyes were gleaming, and days of frustration forgotten. Laurel and Hardy were also relieved. They'd come bearing gifts and the most unlikely item had raised the temperature in the smallest Incident Room they'd ever encountered.

The post-mortem report which came through on the fax confirmed, with only one slight amendment, what the pathologist had said at the scene of the crime. The victim had been stabbed in the back with a large dagger which pierced the heart, but time of death was now thought to be between 9.30 a.m. and 10.30 a.m.

Nigel Fisher arrived at 33, Waterside as requested.

'This can't be pleasant for you, Mr Fisher.'

Byrd approached the matter gently. He knew what he'd gone through the previous day when he realised Stephanie could have been killed, but for this actor a whole world had been destroyed. It had taken him months to come to terms with the tragedy.

'Let me tell you what I know, Mr Fisher. Correct me if I'm wrong.'

Nigel sat glowering at the Superintendent.

'You lived here, I gather, with Sally Siddons for nearly two years, with everything going for you. Then soon after rehearsals for *Romeo* began I understand Sally suffered a personality change and that as a consequence you parted.'

'Aren't you being a shade polite, Superintendent? I was

116

thrown out, on my arse to put it crudely, and all my worldly goods scattered on the pavement.'

The hurt was there, a chasm of pain made deeper by Janet's death. Nigel sat immobile, his jaws clenched, and his eyes firmly fixed on the Magritte print.

'The only way you can help Sally is to talk to me, Mr Fisher.'

'She's dead, so what I say or do makes little difference.'

'Are you saying you don't want the killer caught?'

'How many murderers do you people catch? How many missing persons do you ever find? You don't have to tell me or make excuses. I went down to Scotland Yard and sat there for a whole morning while they waded through records. Hundreds of people vanish each year and are never found.'

Nigel spoke in a monotone, never raising his voice. It was an obituary for a thousand lost souls.

'Mr Fisher, can you actually pinpoint the day on which the relationship between you changed? It could help.'

For the first time the actor looked into the policeman's dark eyes, and answered the prayer he read in them.

'Yes, I can.' His voice trembled as he relived the moment when, twelve months before, rehearsals for *Romeo* had commenced. 'The readings were wonderful. Juliet had several of the cast in tears, and Viv was ecstatic. On the second day Viv blocked the moves, only a preliminary, you understand, because he changes everything as he goes. After the rehearsal on the third day Sally went over the road to the Wardrobe Production Unit to be measured for her costume leaving me to concoct the evening meal, but she didn't return until the following morning. I felt too miserable to eat, left a half cooked meal on the stove, and went to bed.'

'Have you any idea where she went?'

'She didn't tell me, and I never asked. It was that sort of relationship.' He rubbed his forehead as though rubbing would expunge the images from his mind. 'From then onwards everything went downhill. She seemed to spend more and more time with the girls in the wardrobe and less with the company. She even stopped playing Donkey.'

117

He paused in an effort to control himself. 'I . . . I thought for a time she'd fallen for Ben . . . she spent a lot of time with him in the gardens and soon after she threw me out I saw him rowing Sally and Lorraine up the river. Then she stopped socialising altogether and wandered aimlessly on her own. It was during this period that her acting deteriorated. She seemed unable to feel or think the lines . . .' He choked on the words and shook his head. 'Sorry, I thought I'd come to terms . . .'

'Don't rush it,' said Byrd softly. 'This is the first time we've had a clear picture. It will help, believe me.'

'Viv was distraught. I've never seen him like it before. He had to think of the show, of the audience, and the effect Sally was having on us. He couldn't let it go on. He replaced her for the final two rehearsals . . . it was hell for us all . . . we were adjusting to the trauma when her stand-in caught a flu bug. Sally came back. It was miraculous. She suddenly became Juliet, young and innocent, and beautiful. In fact there was something almost scary about her innocence, but she hit the audience and hard bitten critics in the solar plexus. Then, five days later, she vanished.'

'Nigel,' said Mayhew crashing in before he broke down again, 'when were you last here, in the cottage?'

'The night before last,' he whispered. 'The night before Janet died.'

Mayhew glanced towards her boss. An imperceptible shake of his head said *no more questions*.

'After a week of sleepless nights, I called at 33, I needed to talk to someone. Janet too had her problems, and although she wasn't a great communicator I thought we might . . . we might . . .'

'Comfort each other, Nigel?'

'Yes, something like that. She was pleased to see me. We talked into the small hours, drinking red wine and endless cups of coffee. It was odd being here with Janet yet constantly thinking of Sally. The damned crystals had gone, but it was the same furniture, the same picture with inane instructions still . . .'

'Which picture?' Byrd was on his feet.

118

Nigel pointed at the Magritte. The police officers stared at the surrealist painting which afforded them no clues.

'What,' asked Byrd, 'does a bowler hat and a penguin signify?'

'Take it down. Look on the back.'

Stuck on the hardboard were outline drawings of the human figure. The sketch on the top left entitled *The Human Aura* showed the Physical, Etheric, Astral and Mental bodies. The one on the right depicted energy centres, The Crown, Third Eye, Throat, Heart, Solar Plexus, Belly and Root. Two diagrams underneath clearly indicated where to place crystals when practising meditation.

'I shall never know,' said the actor bitterly, 'why Sally believed all that stuff. She had books on the subject too, went into it quite deeply.' He knelt in front of the bookcase. 'That's funny, they're not here. She must have taken them.'

James Byrd could have kicked himself for missing something so blatantly obvious. He wanted the actor out of the way before the same thought hit him.

'Nigel, you'd better be going otherwise Viv will have my guts for garters. You've been frank. You've confirmed our thinking, and we may need to talk again. I'll contact you.'

The actor made his way to the Ashcroft Room knowing he'd missed something. He was practised in recognising changes of mood and speech patterns, it was his job. He was certain Detective Superintendent Byrd was on to something and wanted him out of the way.

As soon as the front door closed Byrd rang Gerald Maitland to ask what he'd done with Sally's belongings when 33 was cleared.

'She didn't leave anything, James. Not a thing.'

'Why didn't she take the picture of a bowler and penguin which hangs over the mantelpiece?'

'Belongs to the RSC, so too does the furniture. Why do you ask?'

'She left behind diagrams, and crystals which I would have thought were important to her, but as she took all her chattels it looks as though she left of her own volition.'

'You think she may still be alive?'

119

'Maybe.'

They'd no chance for further deliberations. The fax started up, and the phone bleeped so they didn't hear the slight plop as another unaddressed envelope fell on the mat. Mayhew saw it first. She picked it up not even bothering to use her handkerchief, the fingerprints would be the same. She handed it to her boss as soon as he'd finished a call from the local station. He ripped it open glaring at her as though she were the culprit.

> Stars hide your fires,
> Let not night see my black and deep desires

'Read it, Sergeant, read the damn thing. It's a confession . . . ' He stopped short thinking of the words he'd heard whispered over Janet's body. 'I wonder,' he said aloud, but Georgina was left guessing. Someone knocking interrupted his train of thought.

The visitor, who was earlier than expected, had parked his recognisable blue Metro well away from the theatre as instructed. It was a useless exercise because as he left the car park he was hailed by Alan Hunt who was clutching a copy of the *Racing Times* and a packet of cigarettes.

'The wanderer returns,' roared Alan as he slapped him on the back. 'What are you doing, chum, trying to get your old job back?'

'No, I am not . . .'

'Oh! So tell me where you've been? Hong Kong, Hawaii, Bali or all three?'

Ben was at a loss . . . just shook his head.

'Come on old chap, tell Uncle Alan all.'

'Alan,' said Ben forcibly, 'you haven't seen me. Got it? You haven't seen me.'

'And why's that old cock?'

'Because the police want to interview me.'

'Interview you!' Alan Hunt stared at him in total disbelief. 'But you weren't here when Janet was . . .'

'Not Janet. About Sally, so the less said about my movements the better.'

'They can't think that you . . .'

'I don't know what they think. That's why I'm here.'

'OK. OK. Keep your hair on. I'll not breathe a word, but let me know what happens. It always helps to get things off your chest.'

Ben half smiled at him.

'You're right. I'm a bit edgy, that's all.' He grabbed the *Racing Times* and waved it above Alan's head. 'Thought you were going to give up the horses and the weed.'

'Not on your nelly – give up my only pleasures – you must be joking.'

As Ben made his way to 33 he wondered why all the subterfuge. Mayhew let him in and waited until her boss had finished reading the faxes before introducing the two men. Ben met the dark eyes of the bearded stranger without flinching. He had nothing to hide. Odd. The policeman reminded him of Walter Raleigh, give him the gear, the ruff and all that and he'd be the spitting image.

Georgina brought him down to earth by recalling the discussion they'd had at Thornton. She was pretty good, left nothing out, canny too.

'You didn't come clean, did you, Ben? There were gaps you didn't fill.'

She was right. He'd been wary. Gut feelings were hardly proof.

'What do you want to know?'

'First of all tell us more about Sally, about how she got involved with the psychic set-up?'

'It started, I think, with two of the girls in wardrobe who were always fooling around pretending they could read the future in tarot cards, or tea leaves, and forever talking about crystals. They'd sit in one of the dressing rooms after rehearsals and fool around, even got our stage manager involved.'

'Lorraine?'

'It's a laugh, isn't it! She's such a strong character, she doesn't need moral support from a pack of cards.'

'Was Lorraine seriously into it?'

'No, because she never had the time. As soon as the show was over she'd be off to her hideout somewhere in the country.'

'I thought she shared a maisonette in Stratford with one of the the assistant stage managers?'

'She does. Has to be on hand for setting up and technicals, but she once told Sally she liked to unwind in the real world, sans actors, sans directors, sans . . .

Byrd interrupted.

'Any idea why Sally and Nigel parted?'

'Nothing tangible. Only crazy notions which shouldn't be uttered.'

'Try me.'

'It'll sound so daft.'

He looked at Mayhew for a lead but she was examining her nails. The policeman with the dark piercing eyes waited.

'It's supposition, nothing more.'

'Go on.'

'Well suppose, when telling her fortune, they were fooling around . . . reading disaster in the cards and in the tea leaves. Sally in some ways was naive . . . suppose they'd gone further and read her hand predicting a broken lifeline, an unsuccessful career, a divorce, bad health . . . black humour, just for a joke? It knocked her flat, and Nigel didn't help. He refused to discuss it, said it was a load of crap.'

'So she talked to you?'

'Only when it was too late, by which time she was heavily into crystals and talked of ridding herself of negative energy. She desperately wanted to believe in herself but doubt and insecurity tore her apart, and in five weeks she'd become a different person. She no longer believed in her own acting talent. Nothing I said made any difference.'

'And Lorraine, didn't she have any influence?'

'Not enough.'

'You were seen with them on the river.'

'Yes, we once took out a boat before wandering into Old Town to look at the wall paintings in the Guild Chapel which was used by the old Grammar School in Shakespeare's day. After that we walked miles. I'd hoped that Lorraine and I could prove to Sally that those stupid

122

girls who'd started it all were wrong, but it didn't work. Lorraine, usually dynamic, was moody, hardly said a word. After that I couldn't take it any more so I left . . . let them think I'd gone abroad.'

He's still in love with her, thought Byrd, and not the joker they all imagined. He delved further.

'Did you know she was a Catholic?'

'Yes. She swapped one creed for another' he said savagely.

'One creed for another?'

'She was naive, for heaven's sake. Being any kind of Christian means an act of faith . . . a leap into the dark accepting unprovable theories. In playing with crystals she went one step further. It was all in the mind. Crystals weren't necessary, any old stone in the road would have done. She could have cleansed it, programmed it, held it in her left hand and hoped for a miracle . . . auto-suggestion would have done the rest. Instead she clutched a rhodonite believing it would give her confidence, self esteem, and help her deal with pressure. Baloney! Sally would have been better off hanging on to her Christian beliefs and leaving the damn stones alone. Sorry,' said Ben quietly, 'I get carried away . . . such a waste, don't you see!'

Byrd saw all right. Nigel and Ben both in love with the girl believed her dead, but three weeks ago she must still have been alive. She'd sent Janet an illegible message on the back of a postcard. What was she trying to say? Was it a warning or a cry for help? He needed much more from this young man, but there was only half an hour before his meeting with Major Drummond and Sir Charles.

'Ben tell me about your job here, tell me about Lenny and the lighting board which is still undergoing rigorous tests.'

'You've seen it?'

'Yes.'

'It's an amazing piece of equipment years ahead of its time.'

'You've operated it, have you?'

'Twice. Once when Lenny was in the theatre, never thinking he'd mind, but he was hopping mad. However,'

Ben chuckled to himself, 'I got my hands on it for a whole morning when he was down at the Barbican.'

'Why are the tests taking such an age?'

'He keeps throwing a spanner in the works.'

'Metaphorically or literally?'

Ben grinned. He liked this man.

'Both. He throws up difficulties when there aren't any and he's not using it to full capacity. He's playing for time.'

'Why?'

Ben was silent. He had no proof . . . could all be in his mind, and his father had warned him to keep his mouth shut.

'We know,' said Mayhew feeling her way, 'that he's sharing his know-how.'

'Sharing it!' Ben was openly scornful.

'Well possibly doing a little business, advising the opposition.'

'Selling the inventor down the river, you mean.'

James Byrd glanced at his sergeant, coded signals passed between them. He took up the questioning playing it low key.

'Have you any idea which facilities aren't being fully used?'

'There may be several, but I came across an interesting programme quite by accident. I'd only a couple of hours, you understand.'

'Go on.'

'There's a lantern on the number one spot bar producing black light, but not the normal type.'

'That's double Dutch to me.'

'Black theatre, which has been going for decades, uses ultra violet light. The most famous Black Theatre company is based in Prague. The actors dress in black, wear black masks and perform against black velvet tabs which means they are totally invisible to the audience. Only objects or clothes painted in UV paint can be seen, rather like cyclists wearing illuminated bands at night. It has a magical quality; a clown can stride across the stage on stilts and look as if he's walking in space. Shoes, gloves and hats can be painted making the actors appear as disembodied wraiths. Children love it, a great gimmick for pantos, but there are drawbacks. The UV lamp needs a considerable warm-up time, and its spread, like any floodlight, is broad but Lenny has his hands on something far more exciting. Viv can't have known otherwise he'd have exploited the possibilities.'

One of Byrd's pleasures in life was watching an artist or craftsman at work be it carpenter, potter or pianist. He was getting a lift from Ben's fascination with his subject. The lad had made a mistake by returning to Merseyside to work within four walls tapping away at a VDU.

'The black light,' said Ben, 'which Lenny could use and never did, makes for superb theatre. For instance, prior to Hamlet's "To be or not to be" speech there would probably be area lighting, but it's now possible to fade out everything leaving the stage in pitch darkness, but as Hamlet commences his speech he can now move into an area where only his face is visible, and with his hands well hidden, seeing only his face would concentrate the audience's attention giving them the feeling they were actually listening to his innermost thoughts.'

'How's it done?'

'By using a remotely controlled infra-red lantern to sense body heat but with the black light source inside requiring minimal warm-up time. It can be focused down to a narrow beam with the black light totally invisible until the actor's face comes into play. It's pre-programmed on the computer which, if necessary, the operator can override with a joy stick.'

'If the lantern is left in position why doesn't someone cotton on?'

'Lenny's made it quite clear that no one's to mess around with any of the new equipment.'

'Off the record, why doesn't he use it?'

As Ben faced the policeman he heard his father's words of warning. *Keep your counsel, son, slander's a heinous offence. You could be had up for defamation of character.* But he had to talk, knew he was right, and he trusted this man, especially with the truth.

'Industrial espionage, it can't be anything else.'

Byrd's smiled as he picked up the swatch of photographs, selected two showing the Japanese full face, and handed them to Ben.

'Have you seen this gent before?'

He gazed at it for some seconds.

'Not sure.' A year's a long time, thought Ben, and they all look the same to me; short with black hair and incredibly fit. 'Sorry I can't help.'

As he handed them back he had a sudden flash.

'Half a minute, there was a Jap sitting in the lighting box with his head well down when we set up *All's Well* last year. Funny that because Lenny hated anyone in the box, said it upset his concentration.'

Byrd had an idea. Instead of keeping Ben's arrival quiet it might produce interesting results to let him be seen, let it be known that he was talking to them.

'Sergeant take Ben over to the theatre, have a coffee in the green-room, let them think he's been to Timbuctoo or wherever, but not a whisper about where he's working now.'

Mayhew looked at him in amazement. This wasn't what they'd agreed. He was doing his own thing again, expecting her to tag along.

'Much better, sir, to stick to our original plan.'

'Reactions are what we need, Sergeant.'

She stood her ground prepared to do battle. She was furious, getting more angry by the second. He saw her jaw tighten, her fists clench but he was in no mood for dissension, his damn leg was itching too much and he might just say things he regretted.

'Stand not upon the order of your going, sergeant, but go at once.'

Ben's laugh broke the tension. 'You really are adopting the Bard, but our short meeting was hardly a banquet.'

A feast of ideas for me, thought Byrd, thankfully.

As soon as they'd left the Incident Room Byrd rang Gerald

Maitland asking for three personnel files to be sent over as soon as possible. Gerald who was in the middle of a meeting with the company manager of Opera North planning a four-week season of opera wasn't too pleased with the interruption.

At the same moment, as Gerald gathered up the files and sped down the corridor towards the stage door, a letter shot through the letter box of 33. The superintendent, who was on his feet in a trice, opened the door and ran into the street in an effort to catch a glimpse of the sender. He was too late, not an actor or technician in sight, only a party of sightseers on a guided tour looking up at the Victorian facade which clothed the Swan and Ashcroft Room. Only the Art Gallery had been left intact after a tempestuous fire on an afternoon in March nearly seventy years before.

A breathless Gerald appeared at the door, thrust files into his hand and was gone again. He threw them on the window-seat and sat down to scan the letter which he handled carefully. A sheet of A4, typed as before, but this time three lines.

> Between the acting of a dreadful thing
> And the first motion, all the interim is
> Like a phantasma, or a hideous dream.

What did it mean? Was the murderer playing with him, or was it an actor's idea of a joke? Someone with a bizarre sense of humour who knew his Shakespeare, or even her Shakespeare? There'd been no time between the acting and the motion in Janet's murder. It had been a sudden vicious thrust. He could do with his old friend Professor Berkeley at his side, a lateral thinker well versed in semantics. This wasn't the last of the anonymous notes, of that he was sure, and Lawrence who was presently occupying the Chair of History at Cambridge might care for a few days in Stratford. He'd call him straightaway. Offer him a challenge.

The Professor who was enjoying his three-year exchange at the university found it far more relaxing than Princeton.

He put that down to the fact that he spent every weekend at Cropredy with Brenda whom he'd married shortly after The Tower case. Two lonely people who needed companionship, who had not expected marriage to offer much more, were rewarded with a deep and satisfying love. For most of Lawrence's fifty-five years an academic life, combined with a love of sport, had filled his days. An occasional affair, not serious enough to disrupt the rutted pattern of his ways. Now his only sport was fishing and his main interest lay in researching and writing historical biographies.

The first six months of married life hadn't been easy. As a single man he'd not been conditioned to a timetable, he'd eaten when he liked, showered when he felt like it, listened to his beloved Beethoven at full blast. Went to bed when he'd had enough of the day, and often rose before dawn to write. Brenda whose late husband had been a Yeoman Warder was used to a regimented life. Breakfast at 7.30 a.m. on the dot, supper at 7 p.m. after The Tower had closed and visitors had departed, and bed never later than 11 p.m. Gradually they developed an easy going understanding. Lawrence played *Ode to Joy* in his study and Brenda the latest pop in the kitchen. Mealtimes became movable feasts which suited Brenda and they retired for the night at 11.30, but Lawrence invariably crept out of bed at 5.30 a.m., made himself a cup of tea, and continued with his writing.

During his first year at Cambridge he'd avenged, in his own inimitable way, the infamous trick Professor Kettle had played on him. Kettle had plagiarised his notes on Francis Bacon, which had taken ten long years research, and then published a monograph in London two weeks ahead of his own Princeton publication. Revenge was sweetly satisfying. When he arrived in Cambridge he lost no time in renewing his acquaintance with Kettle. They shook hands like old friends, and shortly afterwards Lawrence planted predictable seeds by carelessly leaving a briefcase behind his seat at High Table. While he enjoyed a lively debate over coffee Kettle was busy photocopying erroneous information on Monmouth. The plagiarist wasted no time, and strange to relate their two monographs on Monmouth were published the same week. Kettle took a pasting from which he never recovered and Lawrence received the plaudits.

During the night there'd been another note, more a plea, than a warning, thought Byrd.

> Look after her; Remove from her the means of
>   all annoyance,
> And still keep eyes upon her. So, goodnight.

For the first time he felt a real lift. Sally was alive. Find her he would, no matter what the cost. From now on, nothing to the Media, not a whisper, and only basic details for Charlie, the most blessed of all computers, to record. Caution, foreign to his nature, was the answer.

At 10 a.m. an eager policeman arrived to man the Incident Room. Constable Jemmett was keen. This, his first involvement in a murder case, was a lucky break. The Superintendent had made it clear he needed men with computer know-how who could deal with Charlie. Jemmett headed the list.

Only seconds after the constable's arrival another missive dropped on the mat. Byrd, unceremoniously shoved him towards the door.

'Open it man, see where they went.'

Jemmett shaken by this extraordinary welcome looked up and down the road having no clue what he was looking for.

'Where did they go, Constable?'

'Who, sir?'

'Whoever delivered this damn letter.'

'Only saw one person, sir, and she ran into one of those houses further down the street.'

'Which house? You'd better lead the way, and fast.'

Byrd grabbed his walking-stick and followed the trim, uniformed figure of Jemmett who stopped outside a Victorian building.

'It's not a house, sir,'

'No, Constable. It's the RSC's Production Department. You'd better get back to the Incident Room and I'll deal with the little matter of anonymous notes.'

He threw open the door and stood on the threshold listening to the whirr of machines and the chatter of sempstresses. He manoeuvred his way between two rails of costumes which blocked his view. A woman who was pinning a cape on to a doublet had her back to him; all the rest, intent on their work, were unaware of his interest. He was too late. The bearer had seen a uniformed constable enter the Incident Room and had fled to this refuge, or maybe it wasn't a refuge? It could be the normal workplace where he or she would not be missed for the few seconds it took to run up the street. Damn! It could have been anyone. As he walked back to 33 he thought of all the places an actor or technician could have hidden. In vast wardrobes, among costumes hanging on the rails, in the changing rooms. He really should have turned the place upside down.

Jemmett, who'd made himself at home, was feeding Charlie with information.

'There was a call for you, sir, from a Mrs Brown. I said you'd ring back.'

Byrd nodded. A pity he couldn't come clean with Megan Brown. Couldn't even mention the faint possibility that Sally may have been alive three weeks ago. No good raising hopes at this stage. The card could have been written by a joker. The joker, perhaps who was sending these damn notes? He tore the last one open.

But men may construe things after their own fashion.

God Almighty! Wasn't that what he was doing? The damn thing told him nothing. He handed it to Jemmett.

'Fax this to Professor Berkeley, you'll find his number on the pad, and when you've done that take this so-called easy chair upstairs and bring down two hard ones.'

'Yes, sir.'

Byrd wondered whether Lawrence was making any sense of the quotes. Was there a pattern? If there as, he was pretty sure the Professor's devious mind would winkle it out. A man who set such an unlikely trap for Kettle would be able to decode these seemingly obscure words. He'd not entirely approved Lawrence's methods, but he had to admire a man who knew what he wanted and went for it. The Professor's logical approach to problems combined with an insatiable curiosity had proved invaluable on both The Tower and Hampton Court cases. He wasn't surprised when Lawrence leapt at the chance. Trinity term was nearing its end, he'd said, and a week in Stratford would suit him down to the ground. He'd bring Brenda with him, do the job properly, stay at The Moat House with a room overlooking the river. She'd enjoy that.

The Superintendent, desperately needing a cold drink after giving his leg hell in his wild dash to the Wardrobe, was in the kitchen with the tap full on when another letter flew through the letter box. He didn't see the note drop, but Jemmett who was on the phone did. He slammed the phone down, and ran to the front door where he stood for some minutes staring at everyone in the vicinity. No one was running. No one going through the stage door nor entering the Wardrobe. No one hurrying towards the lights at the end of the bridge. Everything looked normal. The only person expending any energy was a young lad with a kite running alongside the river. Never thinking to look down Palmer's Court, the alley-way alongside 33, he quietly closed the door and handed the letter to Byrd.

'Sorry, sir, nothing doing.'

He picked up the phone to find his caller had given up, while his boss sat on a kitchen stool looking totally bemused.

'You all right, sir?'

'I would be, constable, if I could make head or tail of this.'

He read it again.

the report of her is extended more than can be thought to begin from such a cottage. AHC

picture on the top on't

He was angry with himself. The notes, like hail, were coming thick and fast, and his damn leg held him up at every turn. Whoever was sending the bloody things was banking on his infirmity.

'Fax this one to the Professor, Constable, another to add to his collection, ask him who AHC was, and when you've a breathing space don't forget to get rid of the easy chair.'

Sergeant Quinney eased the car round a group of American sightseers who were gazing upwards with their cameras trained on a Victorian edifice. He grinned to himself as he parked alongside a mud bespattered black Metro, thinking about the graffiti he'd scrawl in the dust.

The car park attendant pointed the two Chief Constables in the direction of 33 Waterside.

'Find yourself a coffee, Sergeant, and join us in half an hour.'

'Yes, sir.'

Bob Quinney was far more concerned in examining his own pride and joy than imbibing a cup of coffee. In any case he didn't like the stuff. Always left a nasty taste in his mouth. His boneshaker, as his boss had disparagingly called his VW, was in the best of health. Dickybird had been taking care. But why were the crutches on the back seat, and how was he managing without? He knew his Super. was in for a rough time. The conversation in the car had been guarded, but reading between the lines he realised Major Drummond wanted the Oxford man off the case, wanted someone who was fit, whose image would be more assuasive on the box. Someone who would handle the media with kid gloves.

He waited until his two passengers had been admitted to 33 before he set about decorating Mayhew's car with cupids, hearts and arrows. That would make her mad. Force her to clean it too!

Sir Charles and Fraser Drummond stood in the sitting-room looking at each other in undisguised amazement. Both were speechless. A murder investigation being carried out in an Incident Room no more than 14 ft. × 14 ft.!

132

The only sound was the fax regurgitating its umpteenth message.

Sir Charles gazed at the Magritte. Bizarre, like the whole set-up, then he laughed, couldn't help himself. He avoided the Major's baleful eye by looking through the window. Good God, what was Quinney doing? Bemused he took another look at the Incident Room thinking that this unorthodox officer of his had operated in some strange places.

During The Tower investigation Byrd managed in three small rooms in the Waterloo Barracks not much bigger, come to think of it, than this cottage, but at Hampton Court he'd been provided with princely accommodation in an apartment where Scott of the Antarctic's widow had once lived. This man of his was a pragmatist, he'd make anything work.

'Do be seated, gentlemen,' said Byrd as he picked up a thermos and poured three coffees. It was a tactical move, carefully planned before his adversaries arrived.

Drummond, who was a small man with a shock of grey hair, made the mistake of plonking himself down in the easy chair whose springs were less than supportive. Hardly an advantageous position from which to fire broadsides. He thought about his brief discussion with Sir Charles during the journey. Why had he evaded the issue, never saying yea or nay to the recall of the injured Superintendent? He'd implied it would be ill-considered to change horses in mid-stream. His horse, so he'd said, might be handicapped but had won ninety per cent of his races. It was the other ten per cent that worried the Major. Warwickshire despite its small strength had achieved miracles during the past two years, stumbling across the largest drug consignment ever discovered in the UK, and solving the deadly serial killings. His own men knew how to handle the media. He'd insisted on all his officers attending courses on public relations, an essential part of their training.

By the time he drank his coffee it was cold, and the easy chair belied its name, and he was beginning to get the feeling that his journey would prove a wasted exercise. The Superintendent was managing without crutches which scuppered part of his carefully prepared argument in favour of a change, and dressed in a dark suit but his tie said it all. A jazzy affair in bright blues and greens. More suitable for a radio disc jockey where it would never be seen.

Byrd half smiled to himself at the sight of his adversary deep in that abominable easy chair. One up to Jemmett for his omission.

Sir Charles perched on the window-seat was, as usual, reasonably confident about the case, nevertheless there was no point in putting off the business.

'We're here, Superintendent, to discuss the handling of the case and whether you feel fit enough to carry on with the investigation.'

James Byrd had no intention of handing it over. He'd find the writer of those damned notes if it was the last thing he ever did. He'd find Sally, find the joker who'd tripped him up, and he'd find the murderer. Perhaps writer, joker and murderer were one and the same, but he could say none of this, not even to Sir Charles.

'No slur on your mental abilities,' said Warwickshire's Chief Constable, 'but we must consider whether your present physical disability will impede progress.'

The Superintendent heard the words, innocuous words, which weren't actually saying anything about progress, but everything about his approach to the ravaging hordes of reporters. What Drummond wanted was a presentable figure to front the operation.

He went straight in. He'd nothing to lose.

'Let's forget my leg, sir, which in no way impedes the enquiry. I'm positive the murderer is connected in some way with the theatre. If we solve the case it will be solved here on the spot.'

'She could have been killed by a mugger.'

'She wasn't. It was premeditated. She knew her killer.'

'And Sally Siddons? Do you think the two cases are linked?'

'Too early to say.'

'Early days, as you say, Mr Byrd. Early enough, to hand over to another officer. In my opinion what you need is two weeks sick leave giving you time to recover from your injury.'

Sir Charles intervened.

'Have you made any progress at all?'

'Possibly, sir.'

'Be a little more specific.'

'Give me two days, sir, and if my . . .' *no, intuition was the wrong word for the Major* . . . 'if my reading of the evidence is correct we can make a move.'

'Reading of the evidence,' choked Drummond. 'Are you expecting to make an arrest?'

'Possibly, sir.'

He said nothing. An arrest in two days time would be good news for Warwickshire, it would be foolish to rock the boat.

Sir Charles who realised there was a softening also knew his man, knew his methodology of collecting all the bits of a jigsaw before attempting to assemble them. He'd trusted him in the past; could he trust him in the future?

Fraser Drummond made up his mind.

'Is there anything else you need, Mr Byrd?'

He'd been about to ask, now it was being handed to him on a plate.

'I need Sergeant Quinney for two days in an unrecognisable ramshackle car.'

'No problem there,' said Sir Charles, 'Quinney's just made an awful mess of a black Metro, covered the thing in cupids and hearts.'

James Byrd laughed. The tension of the past hour, gone.

'It's Mayhew's jalopy, she'll be hopping mad.'

Chapter 6

Stars, hide your fires!
Let not light see my black and deep desires.

Mayhew's morning had been entertaining but hardly pro-
ductive. If Dickybird thought his surprise package might
cause turmoil he was barking up the wrong tree. Everyone
was pleased to see the return of the prodigal technician
whom they imagined had done a Marco Polo. Everyone,
that is, except Nigel who studiously avoided shaking hands
or patting him on the back.

Josh emerged from the rehearsal feeling jaded. His age
was telling. He had no longer the enthusiasm or fire to
carry the show on his back. He found himself relying on
Angie, now playing Miranda, whose interpretation of the
role was totally different from Janet's. Angie was a down to
earth young woman always humouring her father whereas
Janet had portrayed her as an innocent girl unaware of
worldly values.

As he crossed the gardens on his way to the Dirty
Duck he heard great gusts of laughter emanating from a
crowd of actors gathered round the woman who'd changed
overnight from a management consultant into a police
sergeant. She was laughing with the rest at a young man.
He couldn't believe it. Later he'd swear his heart actually
stopped. Why hadn't Ben contacted him? Why arrive like
this out of the blue? It still hurt . . . never a word . . .
months of silence . . . not even a phone call, but he'd find
his room as he left it . . . in a mess . . . still full of travel
brochures.

He approached the group slowly . . . didn't want to
make a fool of himself. Above the laughter he could hear
a hundred questions. Did you climb the pyramids? What

136

was Hong Kong like? Were you blessed by the Pope? Did you sail up the Amazon? Did you go round the Horn? Does the Empire State building really shake? And did you walk under Niagara? Josh knew where he'd been, no need to ask fatuous questions.

Gradually the laughter subsided as the actors became aware of Josh standing mute staring at Ben. They moved aside and waited. In two quick strides Ben reached the old actor, threw his arms round him and hugged him as he would have hugged his father.

The actors melted away, quickly, unobtrusively, sadly as they would have done if the scene had been played out on stage, leaving Mayhew with the two men.

Josh tried to hide his emotion by concentrating on the crystal Mayhew was wearing.

'How long will you be staying, Ben?'

'Two or three days,' said Mayhew. 'He's helping with enquiries.'

'Would you like to use your old room?'

'Yes, yes, of course, I would.'

'See you later, then.' Josh hurried away, closeted himself in the gent's loo at the Dirty Duck and wept.

Mayhew hadn't finished. She knew Lenny was in the theatre, and she intended find him.

They traipsed through the wings, up the stairs to the Maintenance Wardrobe which was empty, peered into the Ashcroft Room, down into the Swan Theatre, then into the gallery which was full of tourists on a guided tour looking at the display of busts and portraits of famous thespians including the Bard. Before giving up they decided to take another look in the lighting box. No sign of Lenny or Alan.

'Anywhere else?' asked Mayhew.

'Only the gods which punters call the balcony.'

'Let's try it.'

Georgina found the balcony with its steep rake and lack of light eerie. Ghosts there may have been but no solid flesh. She then followed Ben into the balcony bar. One of the large sliding glass doors was open and on the terrace high above the theatre stood Lenny gazing down on the river which could be seen stretching to the north where it joined the Stratford Canal and south from whence sailed a flotilla of narrow boats.

'The jester returns,' yelled the lighting wizard. 'Good to see you, Ben. Now tell me where you've been.'

'It could be a long boring story.'

'OK. Bore me over a sandwich in the green-room.'

'Alan not around?' asked Georgina.

'No. He's spending the afternoon at Worcester. He'll be putting his money on the 1.30 right now. Loves the gee gees he does.'

Lenny grinned at Mayhew. He was too laid back, too sure of himself. She returned his smile playing along with him, playing along with a man she knew was into industrial espionage.

She looked at the back of his head as she followed him down the stairs wondering whether it was the lure of money that had led him into selling secrets, and how did he find the outlets, or did they approach him? Ordinary people who could fade into the background made the most successful spies, and Lenny, apart from his skill on the board, was certainly ordinary. Needed guts, of course, and motive.

Ben wasn't used to lying, safer to stick to something he knew, so over a cheese sandwich and a cup of coffee, he described Switzerland and Italy, countries where he'd holidayed with his parents. Lenny's pretence at being disappointed because Ben didn't want his job back, was so convincing that the jester felt tempted to call his bluff, but a look from Mayhew told him to hold his peace.

Mayhew left Ben sitting by the river while she returned to the Incident Room to interview Mary and Linda.

Helen, who had a pile of costumes awaiting repairs, which were all needed for the evening performance, was annoyed at losing Mary and Linda, so annoyed that she rang the Incident Room.

'Janet Shaw is dead,' said Mayhew unable to control her anger, 'and we're here to find the murderer before

138

he can strike again. You'll get by with a few snags in your costumes but how will you manage if you lose another leading lady?'

Helen was abject.

'We'll manage somehow, we always do.'

Blonde, blue eyed, dumpy Mary, looking scared, arrived with Linda whose long mousey hair was tied up in one plait at the side of her face, and who was openly curious about why the police wanted to see them.

Byrd who was upstairs lying on the bed resting his leg while he perused the personnel files heard every word. His sergeant had certainly done her homework.

Before Mayhew produced exhibit seven she sat the girls on the two hard chairs then she placed the plastic bag containing crystals on the table between them. She stood behind saying nothing. Linda glanced at the bag with a half smile on her face. What did the lady want? She couldn't know, it had all happened months ago.

The long silence unnerved Mary who began fidgeting with a charm bangle which she twirled round and round her wrist while Mayhew, like Nemesis, waited.

Jemmett couldn't understand why he felt so nervous. The tension was worse than waiting for an opponent to make a lunge which was something he knew about, fencing being his sport. The bangle jangled and the tinny, irritating sound became oppressive.

'For heaven's sake,' said Linda, 'give over.'

'What are we here for?' asked Mary staring hard at Jemmett who didn't react.

'You can't keep us here like this,' said Linda, still quite composed, 'not without asking questions.'

'I think you both know why you're here,' said a quiet voice from behind them.

'If it's the murder,' shrieked Mary, 'it's nothing to do with us. Janet told us not to bother any more.'

'Bother with what?'

'Said it was all hocus pocus.'

'Pick up that bag,' said the sergeant, 'and take a good look at those crystals. Have you seen them before?'

Mary eyed Linda before taking a surreptitious glance at Jemmett who still hadn't moved.

'Well have you?' barked Mayhew.

'Yes,' said Linda nonchantly, picking up the bag and shaking them, 'They were here on the mantelpiece, they belonged to Janet.'

'That's only half the story, isn't it. Janet dug them up from the spot in the Theatre Gardens where you'd buried them.'

Mary covered her face in her hands, and Linda shook. She no longer appeared curious, no longer offhand, she was afraid.

'How did you find out?'

'Mary stuffed a note down the side of a chair. A note, supposedly, written by Sally.'

Constable Jemmett no longer looked like a zombie. He was fascinated. Thankful too that he'd left the tape running.

'These crystals,' continued Mayhew inexorably, 'never belonged to Sally. You bought them, buried them and then proceeded to play the same games with Janet that you'd played with Sally.'

'Oh no we didn't,' said Linda. 'We gave up the tarot cards when Sally vanished.'

'Because you thought you'd gone too far.'

They watched dumbfounded as she took a pack of cards out of her pocket and spread them on the table.

'You played with the Magus, the Star and the Hangman, didn't you?'

'Yes,' faltered Mary.

'And the Priestess, Death and the Devil.'

'Yes.'

'You don't know a damn thing about tarot cards. You think it's a game, and you preyed on the imagination of an unhappy young woman.'

Both girls crumpled, both seemed smaller.

'Who put you up to it?' she shouted.

The two girls looked at each other. They'd promised, hadn't they.

'Well?'

140

'No one,' snapped Linda. 'We were playing around . . . it filled the gaps.'

'What gaps?' yelled Mayhew.

Go easy, go easy, thought Byrd. You've almost got what you want.

'The gaps between performances,' said Linda with her eyes on the floor.

As in response to his prayer the next question was hardly more than a whisper.

'I said, who put you up to it?'

The two girls froze. Mary eyed Linda who put her fingers on her lips. Mayhew wanted to shake the pair of them. She'd reached an impasse and nothing would move them.

The heavy silence was broken by a thud from above. Jemmett almost laughed at the expression on Georgina's face.

'It's the Super.,' he mouthed.

The clumping footsteps above unnerved the two girls. They glanced up the stairs and the first sight they had of Byrd was a plastered foot slowly descending.

'We don't need to detain these two young women, Sergeant. We'll hold them down at the station tomorrow for questioning.'

Mayhew couldn't believe what she was hearing, but it was enough.

'What do you want to know?' screeched Mary.

'It's quite simple,' he said, 'Either you tell us who put you up to all this, the tarot and the crystals, or you can kick your heels down at the station.'

At last Linda came clean.

'My sister was studying crystals for A level and I read the book. It seemed like a fun thing to try, and no harm in it. It's quite easy, you know, to put someone to sleep by swinging a crystal backwards and forwards. We found it fascinating, and then other girls joined in and occasionly one or two of the fellows, but then they all got bored and went back to playing Donkey. That's when Lorraine took an interest; it was she who suggested tarot cards, reading palms, and tea leaves, to add spice, you see. It's true we don't understand the cards, but we had a whale of a time inventing . . .'

'Inventing!' said Mayhew tersely. 'You were vicious. Don't you realise the damage you've done?'

'We didn't mean it,' sobbed Mary.

'So you frightened Sally, told her to leave the theatre, told her she was a failure?'

'That's not true. We'd stopped reading the cards when her mother came to stay.'

'When was that?'

'The day before the first dress rehearsal.'

So that was it, thought Byrd. At last he knew why she'd won unexpected laurels from the Press on the first night.

'Have you finished with them, Sergeant?'

She looked at him bleakly, and nodded. He'd got everything out of them so easily with a simple threat. She'd been too emotionally involved to think straight.

'Get out,' she stormed, 'and don't discuss this interview with anyone, do you understand?'

Jemmet waited until the door had closed on the two girls before handing his Super. a fax from Professor Berkeley.

Arriving late tonight. See you for breakfast in the morning.
A H C Anne Hathaway's Cottage, perhaps?

'Well done, Lawrence, and how idiotic of me to miss it,' he said before passing it to Georgina who was still feeling aggrieved at his intervention, vowing next time she'd take a look upstairs.

Byrd read the situation perfectly but this was no time for apologies. She should be used to his methods by now. He picked up exhibit six.

'Take a look at this postcard of Witley Court, Sergeant. The date is illegible and all we have to go on is olT Fl, at least I think it's an L. Is it a name, or part of a message? FL . . . someone called Flanders, Fletcher, Flood, though I can't for the life of me think of a Christian name ending in OLT. And why the hell didn't she write to her parents? Why write to Janet? What was she trying to tell her? If only I could believe she was alive three weeks ago.'

Mayhew heard the pain.

'It could have been written soon after she vanished, sir.'

'It could.'

'Then we must find the joker who posted it.'

PC Jemmett scribbled down olt Fl and went through the alphabet – bolt – colt – dolt – folt – holt –

'Got it,' he yelled triumphantly. 'It's a pub, sir, Holt Fleet, in the village of Holt . . .'

'Never heard of it,' said Georgina.

'It's near Ombersley where my Gran lives.'

And Ombersley, thought the Superintendent, is near Worcester.

'Well done, Jemmett. How big a place?'

'Only a small village. It's where the Royalists were trying to ford the river after they'd lost the Battle of Worcester. Hundreds of panic stricken fugitives, mostly Scots. There wasn't a bridge, you see, and the Roundhead cavalry pursued them, not giving them a chance. 3000 put to the sword and 10,000 taken prisoner. Holt Castle, where Roundheads were billeted, survived and . . .'

Byrd was interested but this was hardly the time.

'Forget your GCSE, Constable, and tell me whether the castle is occupied.'

'It is, sir.'

'Get down there, Sergeant, right away, nose around, keep in contact. Let's hope we're not too late.'

'Right, sir.'

'Take a wet cloth with you. You'll need it.'

'What!'

'I don't understand. What are you saying?'

'You'll see, Sergeant, you'll see.'

She did see. She might have been amused if she hadn't been in such a hurry, but she had to clean the damn thing. Quinney's hieroglyphics made her small insignificant car immediately memorable.

It was a spur of the moment decision. A feeling that the

143

quotations were coming to an end, but more than that he wanted to see where Anne Hathaway had lived. Shottery wasn't far, would only take him ten minutes to get there.

He read the message again.

> *the report of her is extended more than can*
> *be thought to begin from such a cottage. AHC*
>
> *picture on the top on't.*

Why the gap between the lines. and what was 'picture on the top on't' telling him? Not pictorial if the joker was following a pattern. It would have to be another envelope, another quote. 'Imagine a letter on top of it', might make sense?

At the end of an eight-minute journey he met with double yellow lines which he ignored. There was no way he was going to walk from the official car park, his leg, hot and itching, was giving him hell. He stuck a note under the windscreen wiper and made straight for the house not bothering to queue at the ticket kiosk. A middle aged grey haired guide checked an identity card proffered by a tall bearded policeman, and then proceeded to show him over the farmhouse. The guide was adamant that nothing could be hidden in the upper rooms which were roped off, nevertheless Byrd climbed up the narrow wooden stairs, and down again, cursing his infirmity. Not an envelope in evidence. His last hope, if it was anywhere, had to be the kitchen. Both men looked in the inglenook, in the bread oven, in the cauldron, behind the fire-irons and under the wood.

A young female guide was explaining to a group of Americans that pot luck in Anne Hathaway's day meant exactly that. Meat, vegetables, poultry and bread were all chucked into a cauldron, which hung suspended over a constant fire, to provide sustenance at any time of the day. One of the visitors, a blue haired elderly woman, was more interested in the court cupboard.

'How much would something like this cost today?' she asked.

'Thousands, though you could buy a reproduction here in Stratford.'

The American shook her head, she wanted the real McCoy.

The ancient piece of furniture was his last hope. He eased his way through the crush of bodies and with his hand well above his head felt along the top surface of the court cupboard.

'Eureka!'

He waved it at the grey haired guide who was intrigued and now agog to see what was written, but the policeman, who'd no intention of sharing the spoil, thanked him and made his way back to the car.

It was the longest message yet and, intuitively, he knew it was the last.

> O, God help me! God help me!
> how long have you professed apprehension?
>
> . . .
>
> I fear a madness held me and do entreat Thou
> pardon me my wrongs

He didn't need a concordance, didn't need to know from which plays the words were borrowed. He didn't need Lawrence to decode this message. He shivered slightly. It could be a last desperate call for help before a reluctant murderer selected his next victim. Back to the Incident Room pronto and fax this to Cambridge in case the Professor could come up with a mental picture of the writer.

It took Mayhew half an hour to reach Holt. As she drove over the bridge she thought of Charles II escaping northwards, hiding in an oak tree before making his escape to France leaving thousands of slaughtered countrymen dead on the battlefield. She saw the weary infantry soaked to the skin following in his wake; a disillusioned army of Scots who never saw their homes again.

Once over the bridge she found parking on the forecourt of Holt Fleet. The inn, adjacent to the river, stood four square as Jemmett had described. She found a gardener,

145

with beads of sweat on his brow, trying to mow an almost vertical patch of grass alongside the bridge with a Flymo. Sisyphean, she said to him but he stared at her as though she'd just dropped in from another planet. He knew enough, just enough to give her directions to Witley Court, but he knew nothing about Holt or Holt Heath. He was an Ombersley man, lived three miles away, but it could have been 300, thought Georgina dismally.

Witley Court at the end of a rutted puddled lane was not what she expected. The postcard depicted a palatial edifice as it stood in 1870 with its formal gardens and monolithic fountain in the foreground. Jemmett could have saved a lot of time if he'd explained it had been destroyed by fire in the 1930's and was now a magnificent monumental ruin scandalously vandalised. Fortunately, after nearly fifty years of neglect, English Heritage had stepped in to save it for the nation.

There were very few people around, boring for the young man in the ticket booth who lived locally and who liked to chat up visitors. She let him elaborate on the ruin which in its heyday had been the playground of princes and playboys, all those who'd had leisure enough to indulge in hunting, fishing, and wild parties culminating in other pleasures of the flesh, and on occasions producing untitled, unrecognised descendants.

'See the church, madam, it's something you mustn't miss.'

First she walked through the shell imagining the gilded plasterwork, the handwoven Persian carpets, exquisite statuary, crystal chandeliers, and elegant Georgian and Victorian furniture which had clothed the interior. Then she stood under the portico at the top of a flight of steps looking down on a vast sweep of lawn where formal gardens once charmed the eye and assailed the senses. To her right was the orangery, its black and white marble tiled floor looking much as it would have done nearly 200 years ago. Even the wires which had once supported the grapevines were still in evidence. Another life, she thought for the privileged few, at the expense of the ordinary man. She decided to take a quick look in the church, the finest baroque parish church in the kingdom, the ticket man had said. Laying it on a bit thick, she thought.

She opened the outer door and closed it as the legend instructed. There was nothing remarkable about the doors leaving her totally unprepared for the glorious vision which devastated her as she entered the church. She was there alone. Breathless. Exhilarated. All this beauty to herself. Italianate ceiling paintings. Sumptuous stained glass windows. Elaborate gilded plasterwork. The glorious feeling of space uplifted her spirits. Suddenly she thought of Sally. Is this where she bought the postcard of Witley Hall? Had she been here?

She found the cards at the back of the church. There! There it was, the selfsame picture. Witley Court in 1870. Only 10p. She hastily bought a couple, placed her contribution in the box, and hared back to the attendant. She had a great deal to ask him.

It was too much to hope for. No, he didn't remember seeing a young lady with hazel eyes and long dark tresses. Neither on her own, nor with a friend. Very few people came alone, except artists, of course, who arrived with all their gear to spend three or four hours sketching the place.

'It's thanks to artists,' he said, 'that we know what the place looked like in 1800 with its black and white cottages and medieval church. They moved it, you know.'

She looked at him blankly.

'Moved it!'

'The church. It now stands in Holt village.'

'You mean they took it down and rebuilt it stone by stone?'

'That's right, miss, but it wasn't so difficult when it came to the cottages, timber framed, you see. They stripped them and moved the frames on low loaders almost 170 years ago.'

'What!' Mayhew was appalled. 'You mean the lords of the manor removed the unfortunate peasants, willy nilly?'

'They did too, turned the manor house into a palace, you see.'

Mayhew was incensed.

'Lording it over the serfs.'

'Yes, miss, but those cottages still stand and people still live in them which is more than you can say for the palace, so they didn't do a bad job.'

She thought of a mother with seven or eight children being uprooted, her few precious belongings loaded on to a cart which her husband, if he was allowed the time, pushed to the next village. Uprooted as easily as a bush planted in the wrong spot. She calmed down. What good was anger 170 years after the event?

'You should take a look at the thatched cottage which stands hidden among the trees above Holt Fleet, that's the pub by the river.'

She half smiled.

'I might just do that, and thanks.'

How strange, thought Mayhew, as she walked back to her car that the twentieth century attendant should so readily accept the indignities suffered by villagers at the beginning of the nineteenth.

Before returning to Stratford, her mission having produced damn all, she'd definitely take a look at the cottage. Moving house had taken on a whole new meaning.

As Byrd eased himself out of the car he noticed the car park attendant reading *The Racing Times*. From somewhere in his subconscious there was a slight fluttering of an idea. Anything, no matter how way out, was worth trying. A laughable idea. Nothing he could share. He'd get Jemmett to fax the latest cryptic message to the Professor, before sending him out to buy a couple of sports papers.

Stephanie, who'd not been allowed to return to work, wasn't surprised when James rang to say he'd be late. Par for the course. She'd spent the afternoon weeding and dead heading roses which hadn't helped ward off the shakes. She felt totally incapable of making a decision, even a simple thing like shopping. She couldn't face it. Kate would have to nip round to the village store after school. The following week would be unbearable, she'd be on her own while Kate was in France on a school trip.

148

Being on her own was scary, she'd never felt so insecure before, but Doctor Elliott had assured her the feeling would wear off in a few days, and she'd be as right as rain. Get your mother over, he'd said, but James would never wear that.

Bob Quinney drove back to Stratford in a battered, dark blue Montego with a souped up engine that Mansell would have appreciated. His boss who'd not been eased off the case sounded ebullient. Told him to be prepared for a long evening. Just like old times.

During Mayhew's absence Byrd settled down to read *The Racing Times* before switching on the TV to watch the 3 o'clock from Worcester.

While the racing was on an exuberant Gerald Maitland dropped in to hand over the list Byrd had requested. His discussion with Opera North had born fruit resulting in a month of Verdi being set up in the main house. He was an enthusiastic opera buff, and Verdi above all kept him sane. After a frantic twelve hour day in the theatre he'd retire to his small bachelor flat in Leamington Spa well away from the madding crowd, and play a CD. *Un Ballo in Maschera* accompanied by a stiff cognac left him feeling relaxed.

'Sorry, James, I was up to my eyes when you rang, but I've got what you wanted and more.' He fished in his pocket. 'Here's the list of the problems which arose during the production of *Romeo and Juliet* last year, all gleaned from the deputy stage manager's file.'

Byrd cast his eye over the large black scrawl.

1 *Band parts for the instrumentalists missing.*
2 *Wigs all too small. Original order form lost.*
3 *Paris's turquoise codpiece missing on opening night.*
4 *2nd performance Tybalt's dagger and rapier mislaid*
5 *Deputy Stage Manager's prompt-script vanished on the morning of the final Dress Rehearsal.*
6 *Juliet's ball dress ripped.*

'Are most shows beset with these sort of problems?'

149

'No. There are alarms and excursions but nothing on this scale, except . . .'

'Yes?'

'Viv is experiencing quite a few ups and downs with *The Tempest*.'

That was all the policeman needed.

'Do you know where Lorraine parks her car?'

'Down the road.'

'Could you take Bob with you and point it out.?'

Gerald did a double take.

'You're not thinking that she's . . .'

'I've an open mind, but we need to check.'

And that's all Gerald could get out of him. He and Quinney made their way along Waterside towards The Other Place where she parked during the day, unless there was a matinée. Gerald agreed to call the Incident Room as soon as the rehearsal was over to keep them informed about Lorraine's movements. Quinney then parked the Montego at the end of Waterside where it became a one way street.

Lawrence was worried. Breakfast with James might be too late. He'd get over there straight away, collect Brenda *en route* and they could be in Stratford by teatime. At least the hotel was expecting them.

Brenda took the quiet route across country while he sat and concentrated on the quotations which he'd noted down in the order they'd been received. A strange pattern emerged. An unpredictable pattern, but wasn't human nature like that? Almost cocking a snook at the police to begin with, or at one particular policeman, then a surprising volte-face by providing information followed by a distinct avowal of fear. Why? What had the sender to fear?

It was a hot steamy afternoon and as the door to the Incident Room was wide open the professor, not bothering to knock, stepped right inside. Byrd, who saw the expression on Jemmett's face, turned to find Lawrence whose hair was greyer and longer than ever smiling down on him.

150

'Lawrence, you old rogue, good to see you. This is a bit early for breakfast isn't it?'

'Couldn't leave it any longer, James. That last message is dynamite.'

'Yes. It leaves me feeling powerless and uneasy.'

'Have you been tripping the light fantastic?' asked Lawrence staring at the plaster.

'I didn't trip, I fell, but that's a story that can wait. Why don't we walk round to Hall's Croft and have a cup of tea. There we won't be disturbed.'

'Tell me about Hall's Croft,' said Lawrence as they cut through New Place Gardens.

'It was the home of Shakespeare's favourite daughter Susanna who married a Dr John Hall. The original early sixteenth-century house was enlarged in the seventeenth, probably by Dr Hall himself, and again in the eighteenth and nineteenth which weakened the structure. However the Birthplace Trust did a splendid job in the 1950's. You'll love it. An impressively furnished Tudor house.

They made their way to the far corner of the tearoom after ordering home-made scones and a large pot of tea.

'It seems to me,' said the Professor, 'that your case has much to do with the Bard.

There are more things in heaven and earth, Horatio,
Than are dreamt of in your philosophy.'

Lawrence laughed.

'I am not a philosopher so enlighten me.'

'There are so many people dissembling, people who know why a lapsed Catholic lass is missing.'

'Shakespeare dissembled all his life, so what's new?'

'Had to, didn't he, and you will know whether my reading of the situation is correct. His parents were ardent uncompromising Catholics living in an age when persecution reached new heights. Who could prove the poet wasn't also a recusant? Despite all the constrictions I believe Will was married at Temple Grafton by a Catholic

151

priest who'd been left in peace only because Anglicans despised him for his inability to preach. Our poet was an astute man, keeping a low profile when his cousins Catesby, Winter and Tresham became involved in the Gunpowder Plot. Other relations were hanged, drawn and quartered, and his Catholic sponsor Henry Wriothesley, Earl of Southampton, was kept a close prisoner in The Tower.'

'He kept his head, my friend, because he lived in Cripplegate with the Mountjoys, a Huguenot family who were exempt from the obligation of attending the Anglican Church. You'll find names of his fellow actors at Southwark proving they received Communion but never, ever, William Shakespeare.'

'Yet he became a lay-rector here in Stratford. Was that a smokescreen or did he see a different light?'

'We shall never know, but I guess we'd better get down to the nitty gritty and not get immersed in the Bard's problems.'

Lawrence, whose exposition was fascinating, did the talking.

'I think,' he said, 'that the first message

> To mourn a mischief that is past and gone,
> Is the next way to draw new mischief on

is telling you to keep your hands off the case. In other words stop looking for Sally Siddons otherwise she's in danger. Then you have three more warnings followed by a confession,

> Between the acting of a dreadful thing, and the first motion,
> all that interim is like a phantasma or a hideous dream.

After that another three or four quotes telling you to keep off then we have

>Stars hide your fires!
>Let not light see my black and deep desires

This is scary, a distinct warning, then the penultimate instruction to go to Anne Hathaway's Cottage.'

'But why?'

'To get you running. Someone who knows you have a game leg, someone who wants to cause you physical and mental stress.'

'Man or woman?'

'A woman, I'd say, with a chip on her shoulder.'

'And the final note, Lawrence, the one that leaves me shit scared?'

'It's the first time she's not given you a verbatim quotation. "O God help me" is from *Much Ado*, but the final sentence is a mishmash from *The Tempest* because she couldn't find an apposite quote. It's from Act Five, Scene One, starts at line 116, "I fear a madness held me", then she picks it up again a couple of lines later with "and do entreat Thou pardon my wrongs". It's the final quote, James. She can say no more.'

Who, thought Byrd, was brilliant at Donkey? Who knew *The Tempest* backwards in her sleep?

'God help me, Lawrence, I hope I'm in time.'

The two men left Hall's Croft. The bearded policeman went to the Incident Room and the American made his way through the car park to the river thinking he preferred solving ancient mysteries where there was no price to pay if his premise was wrong.

While he stood cogitating Brenda was having her hair washed and blow-dried before embarking on a shopping spree, a ploy in which her husband had no intention of being involved; much better acquaint himself with the Bard's birthplace. The tall, grey haired man with a loping stride quickly covered the short distance from Waterside to the half-timbered sixteenth-century house in Henley Street.

He joined a throng of cosmopolitan sightseers who were queuing patiently at the Shakespeare Centre. He

153

marvelled as he often did at the genius of a Stratford lad educated in a local grammar school less than half a mile away from home, whose talents produced thirty-seven recognised plays and possibly many more disputed texts.

As he stood in the room where John Shakespeare, a glover and wool dealer had plied his trade, he thought of his young son playing on the same stone laid floor over which millions had trod causing it to become smooth and shiny. The man who had such a way with words, who understood the human condition was still alive in the house, as alive in the house as he was in the theatre.

Lawrence followed a crowd of excited French school-children up the stairs to the bedroom. While they sur-rounded the plain wooden bed he turned his attention to the latticed windows and was devastated to find that vandals had etched their names into the ancient glass. He knelt on the floor to take a closer look and was amazed to discover that the culprits were none other than Sir Walter Scott and Sir Henry Irving whose leading lady, Ellen Terry, had also made her mark. Charles Scrivener, an American publisher, was another name he knew well, and Isaac Watts in 1748 was the earliest he could find.

The young French scholars departed leaving him in peace to survey the quilt covered bed. He would have liked to examine the ropes stretched across the frame used to support blankets and sheepskins which would have served as a mattress. The ropes had to be tightly secured otherwise Mary Shakespeare and her infant son would not have *slept tight*.

He wandered downstairs trying to imagine the meta-morphosis which took place when in the early nineteenth century the house became an inn. The landlord of the Swan and Maidenhead swore that when he relaid one of the floors he discovered wool combings embedded in the foundations. Wool combings left from the trade followed by John Shakespeare.

Lawrence had an overwhelming desire to communi-cate with the Bard . . . tell him what was happening at the theatre . . . how his words were being borrowed to describe a tragedy which might happen at any moment.

154

A bizarre desire, but the circumstances were dramatic enough to form the basis for a drama. A young and beautiful girl missing, another murdered, the attempted murder of a policeman, and industrial espionage not unknown to Walsingham the great Tudor spymaster. Shakespeare would have had a field day.

He strolled back to the hotel down the High Street where he stopped to gaze at Harvard House, another architectural gem, rebuilt after a fire in 1596. Katherine Rogers had lived there, Katherine the mother of John Harvard who founded the first American University. What a pity the roof was tiled, it would look so much better thatched.

Gerald Maitland rang to say the rehearsal was over but Lorraine, who was sorting out props with her assistant stage managers would be some time. As soon as they got the message the two policemen made their way to the battered Montego and sat waiting. It was a long wait, but far from boring because Quinney who was knowledgeable about racing, and an avid reader of novels by Dick Francis, kept his boss amused.

It was 7 o'clock before Lorraine left Stratford. She didn't hang about. Straight to Droitwich, carefully through the town, and onwards to Ombersley. It was only as she picked up the A433 to Holt Heath that she realised the dark blue Montego had been behind her for miles. She took a good look in the mirror at the driver who was mouthing something. Singing to himself, she thought. Nothing to worry about, but she did worry. Getting paranoid, she told herself. The car behind had taken a strange route, unless the driver was a local man and knew all the back doubles as she did. Another look before she crossed the bridge. Good, she was on her own now, the car had gone. She breathed more easily, pulled off the road and parked in front of the pub.

As she ran into the bar she glanced through the window just in time to see the Montego parking alongside a white Transit. She caught a glimpse of a passenger in the back seat wearing a flat cap and dark glasses. She'd know him anywhere. She shivered. Why was she afraid?

She'd committed no crime. There was no way they could pin anything on her . . . nothing illegal, but she knew it would come to this. Had always known. She was a fool, she should have destroyed the evidence, but there was no time, all she could do now was remove it. The two men in the car remained seated, as she thought they would, waiting for her to emerge. Let those two clever gits sit there. She was one step ahead.

The landlord poured her a half lager, as usual, which she placed on the table near the window. As usual. She then rummaged through her handbag, found a biro and left it alongside the unfinished *Guardian* crossword.

The regulars in the bar thought nothing of it when she made her way to the Ladies loo, nor did they see her as she slipped quietly away through the back exit. Clambering up the precipitous hill on an uneven path for nearly half a mile left her gasping. She stopped for some minutes to get her breath back, and as she did so Canada geese, better than any watchdogs, warned the neighbourhood that an enemy approached. She could see the small chalet hidden from the road on one side by an ancient hedge, and on the other by the Strachan's thatched cottage. She approached it carefully in case they'd changed their plans and returned home from a motoring holiday in France earlier than expected, which is what had happened the previous year. They were obviously not in residence because wild ducks were practising taking off and landing on the swimming pool.

The back door of the chalet was ajar. She ran straight into the kitchen expecting to find supper ready, something they'd have to forego. Odd! Nothing on the stove. No appetising smell. No table set. Then panic. Utter panic.

'Sally!' she screamed. 'Sally, where are you?'

Trembling she stood listening to the silence. She could swear there was someone in the house, but why didn't Sally answer? God! Was she dead? She opened the sitting-room door expecting the worst but what she saw stopped her in her tracks. Sally sat there facing her. Doing nothing. Saying nothing. Staring straight ahead. Lorraine didn't know whether to be angry or overjoyed.

'For God's sake, Sally, you don't have to act the Tragic Muse. You gave me a hell of a fright. Quickly, get your things together, we're leaving.'

Why wasn't Sally looking at her? She was focusing on something beyond. Lorraine turned and stood transfixed.

'My God,' she whispered it's you!'

'Yes,' said Mayhew. 'It's me.'

'You've got nothing on me,' yelled Lorraine. 'No kidnap. No murder. Sally is here because she wants to be here.'

'I doubt that,' said the Superintendent as he entered the room followed by Quinney. Byrd had been in contact with Mayhew from the moment she'd seen Sally leaving the small chalet on the far side of the swimming pool to gather herbs.

The Strachans pining for home and worrying about the geese, the hens and the dogs had returned early, as they always did, despite the fact that Sally had promised to feed the animals. Mayhew had found the Strachans in the garden sunning themselves, and when they learnt she was fascinated with the history of the cottage they were only too eager to show her round.

She lovingly stroked the beams that 170 years before had withstood the shock of being unceremoniously relocated. The cottage standing four square at the top of the hill could have been there since Tudor times. No one would ever have guessed at its chequered history.

It was while she was looking out of one of the bedroom windows that she saw Sally Siddons emerge from the chalet at the far side of the swimming pool and make her way to the herb garden. She called Byrd who'd only just arrived at the pub at the bottom of the hill to give him hurried directions before organising the Strachans who put the deck-chairs away and closed all the curtains. Ted Strachan had opened the back door for the two policemen while Mayhew comforted a startled young actress whose hands were full of marjoram and thyme.

Byrd looked with distaste at the stage manager who'd caused such chaos in the theatre and so much unhappiness for the Browns. He wanted to wipe that contemptuous expression off her face.

'You're crazy,' she said, 'if you think she was kidnapped.'

'I wonder, Miss Jefferson, whether you're satisfied with your vicious evil work?' You've tried to destroy this girl. You've demoralised her, taken control of her mind for your nefarious purposes, and coerced her into a situation where she's a virtual prisoner.'

'She's no prisoner,' said Lorraine softly, 'and you know it. No windows locked. No doors bolted. No need, you see, because she keeps herself to herself.'

'No pity either,' rasped Byrd, 'for her parents who don't know whether she's alive or dead.'

'They know I'm alive,' said Sally. 'I write every week.'

'And where do you post them?' asked Mayhew sitting beside her and taking her hand.

'Lorraine buys the stamps and posts them on her way to the theatre, but they're never answered,' she said sadly.

'It's an indictable offence, Miss Jefferson, to interfere with the passage of Royal Mail.'

'That's something else you'll have to prove, isn't it?'

'You weren't careful enough,' said Mayhew, 'which I find surprising in a stage manager. You screwed up the letter Sally wrote last Sunday and dumped it in your neighbour's dustbin.'

For the first time Lorraine was at a loss for words. She sat down and clenched her fists. She'd wanted this to end. She'd thought of so many ways. It had got on top of her, but she couldn't bring herself to . . .

'No,' she cried, 'this shouldn't have happened, not like this.'

Byrd remembered what she'd said when she stood over Janet's corpse.

'This shouldn't have happened,' he repeated. 'That's what you said once before. You're in too deep Miss Jefferson.'

Lorraine moaned quietly, for herself, not for her victim.

'Georgina,' said Byrd. 'Take Sally home. Her mother's

expecting her, and at this stage nothing to the Press. I'll deal with that in the morning.'

'Come on,' said Mayhew gently, 'I'll collect my car from up the lane while you pack you bits and pieces.'

Sally didn't make a move.

'My parents,' she said, 'are they all right, and do they really want to see me?'

'Of course they want to see you. This will be the most joyful day of their lives.'

Sally smiled, a radiant smile which lit her face warming the hearts of the three police officers. This, thought Byrd, makes everything worth while, the sort of experience he'd miss when he gave up the job.

'Well,' said Lorraine, when the two women had gone, 'accuse me, indict me, do what you have to do, and get it over.'

Byrd was quite sure in his own mind that this was no lesbian liaison, but he wanted to know why and to do that he was prepared to intimidate and threaten.

'First of all, Miss Jefferson, let's discuss attempted murder, an indictable offence in my book.'

She was belligerent.

'What the hell are you talking about? I've never tried to kill anyone in my life . . . I . . .'

She trembled remembering the iniquitous thoughts that had troubled her for so long. Thoughts that so easily might have fathered the deed but, thank God, they hadn't.

'But you were an accessory, an accessory to the attempted assassination of a police officer.'

The grim face of the man questioning her said it all . . . there was no way out. She felt sick.

'It was a joke. That's what Lenny said. All I did was ring him when you left Wardrobe Maintenance.'

'Letting the trap down was a joke?'

'It was only meant to go down a few inches, just enough to give you a jolt. I truly believed him, that's why I switched the torch on and off to get you upstage.'

'So Lenny took it down.'

'I think so, but he was in the box when you fell.'

'Of course he was! How stupid.'

159

Quinney and Mayhew looked at him wondering what was stupid, while Byrd suddenly visualised the whole scene from the lighting box. With the black light operating Lenny followed his progress across the stage, and once he'd fallen directed Lorraine, over the speakers, to place a stage weight beside him, but, and this was what he'd not foreseen, someone else had lowered and raised the trap. At last the jigsaw was coming together, but there were still large pieces missing.

'Lenny told you to pick up the stage weight.'

'Yes.'

'You were set up. If I'd been found dead it would have been your word against his.'

She shivered. It was something she'd realised from the start.

'Why did you do it?'

'Because I thought Lenny guessed where Sally was. He never said but . . .'

'He might have foiled your next despicable plan?'

'Yes.'

'Now perhaps you'll explain why you've set about disrupting Viv Mollington's productions.'

'Because I could do his job, and do it a damn sight better, but I'll never get the chance. His training was the same as mine. A degree in drama and English at Birmingham, except I gained a first, he only managed a second.'

Quinney who knew nothing of internecine struggles in the theatre found it difficult to believe that ambition and jealousy had resulted in one actress being spirited away and another murdered. He tried to concentrate on what she was saying.

'I soon realised my forte was production. Proved it didn't I! When Viv was down at the Barbican and his assistant in hospital with appendicitis I carried on with the production and made noticeable improvements. Even Josh said that. Now all I do is stage manage and take boring understudy rehearsals. I can do the bloody job but he never listens, never gives me a chance.' Her voice trailed away.

'So you played psychic games with naive unsuspecting young women?'

160

'Linda and Mary were into crystals in a big way and quite by accident I discovered they were easily influenced. Child's play which opened a door. I persuaded them to try tarot cards and other methods of fortune-telling because I'd dreamt up a way of destroying Viv. It was easy. He wanted me to stage manage his productions which gave me the chance to do maximum damage. Mary and Linda never understood what was happening. They were as naive as the rest.'

Byrd let that pass. He knew they had an inkling otherwise why stop fooling around with tarot cards after Sally vanished?

'But your Svengali methods didn't work with Janet.'

'They did for a time because she quickly became unsure of herself. Doubted her own abilities and when an actress does that she's finished.' She gave a harsh laugh. 'Viv was tearing his hair out, Josh was more irascible than ever, and Nigel was distinctly edgy. That's why Viv brought you lot in. Soon after your arrival, and I'll never know why, Janet became positive again about her acting, and chucked the crystals out.'

'I'll tell you why. By using crystals, as they're meant to be used, Sergeant Mayhew restored her confidence.'

'Good old Georgie,' breathed Quinney.

Lorraine closed her eyes seeing herself thwacking the door so hard she expected it to cave in. She'd wondered at the time how Janet had managed to sleep through the din. That damned woman, that Jackie Kennedy lookalike, was in the cottage with her. She'd noticed the crystal round her bloody neck, never dreaming she practised crystallomancy. Didn't seem the type. Damn her!

'So, Miss Jefferson, you set out to destroy the RSC.'

'No. No, of course I didn't. I love the place. Viv was my target. Other directors, other productions would succeed, but Viv would go down.'

She closed her eyes – wouldn't look at him.

'It couldn't go on. You were getting desperate having started something which you'd never thought through. To begin with you thought yourself clever with your ingenious quotes, but your final throw was an SOS. You were afraid

161

to produce Sally knowing you'd never work in the theatre again, and you hadn't the stomach to finish the game.'

She opened her eyes, and whispered something he found difficult to catch. He thought she said *I'd grown fond of her*.

Byrd looked at the face of evil. A woman driven by an overpowering ambition to succeed in a man's world. A handful of women had made it, among them Joan Littlewood down at Stratford East, and a sprinkling had been invited on rare occasions to direct at the RSC, but never a woman in a commanding position.

He'd not the remotest chance of pinning a kidnapping charge on her, and with a clever defence counsel she might even wriggle out of the charge of destroying Royal Mail.

'Return to Stratford, Miss Jefferson, stay put, and keep away from the Press. You won't have a job in the morning, but I need you on call.'

'I had nothing to do with Janet's murder . . .'

'Not directly, but I hope you have it on your conscience for the rest of your life.'

Megan Brown was nervous, so nervous she forgot to put sugar in the egg custard. Sally was safe, her prayers answered, but where had she been? Who had abducted her, and was she harmed in any way? George, assuming a composure he didn't feel, tried to calm his wife who'd not sat for the past two hours, not since she'd heard the news.

'Don't cry, Megan. She mustn't see you like this.'

He was right, she should be laughing not crying.

'Here, try this.'

He handed her a swab of cotton wool soaked in witch hazel which she held against her eyes. It was blessedly cool.

'That's better, love. Now sit down and have a gin and tonic.'

She'd barely had time to pull herself together when Mayhew rang the bell. Only then did George's apparent calm dissolve. Before Megan could get out of the chair, he'd rushed to the door and flung it open.

He stared at his daughter for some seconds not able

to speak, frozen in time. For one awful moment Megan thought he was going to have a stroke, but he stood there not moving a muscle as Mayhew gave Sally a gentle push up the step and into her mother's arms.

'Mum,' whispered Sally, 'Oh Mum it's great to be home.'

The years dropped away. Megan remembered her daughter as a ten-year old running home from school screaming because she'd lost her satchel. She'd stepped into the hall and they'd hugged each other in the same way, in the same place. It was too much for George. He went into the kitchen and wept, the trauma of the past year too great a burden, the strain of never daring to voice his thoughts, continually supporting Megan in her wild fancies.

'Lord forgive me, forgive me my doubt.'

Mayhew quietly closed the door and walked down the garden path feeling choked. There should have been champagne flowing, bells ringing, dancing in the streets celebrating the return of a lost daughter. Joy? Yes, there was joy, but sadness too, the suffering of the past year had left its mark, could never be forgotten.

Quinney drove slowly back to Stratford, back to the Incident Room knowing that while they were at Holt his boss had solved part of the equation, but he realised from Byrd's odd snatches of tuneless humming that he wasn't quite there.

Jemmett had gone off duty and been replaced by Constable Shaw who was thumbing his way through *Exchange and Mart* when he heard a key turn, and the door open. He sprang to attention but a tired Byrd waved him into the kitchen and told him to put the kettle on. Much to Quinney's surprise his boss grabbed the *Racing News* and sat on the window seat studying it intently.

'Any one in your mob keen on racing, Constable?' he yelled.

'I'd say there's three who go for a laugh and a day out, and Inspector Hart who's a fanatic.'

'Good. When you've made the tea call Inspector Hart and tell him I'd like to see him here as soon as possible.

Quinney knew better than to ask why, all would be made clear.

When James Byrd arrived home Stephanie was in bed fast asleep with Kate lying open-eyed beside her.

'Mummy was cold,' she whispered.

'Has she taken the tranquillizers?'

'Yes.'

'Good. You stay there, my darling, until I've had a bath and then we'll play musical beds.'

Kate giggled. Stephanie stirred and moaned softly. Byrd put his fingers on his lips.

'Daddy, don't go.' He stopped and crept back to the bed. 'Mummy says I can have a rabbit if you'll make a hutch.'

She looked at him anxiously.

'You will, won't you?'

'Yes, darling, as soon as this case is over.'

She was satisfied with that, and cuddled up to her mother again.

Before pouring himself a stiff whisky, more necessary than a bath, he rang his mother-in-law in Abingdon. She wasn't his favourite person, but he had to admit there was no one quite like Laura when it came to coping with a crisis. She listened and she agreed. He was satisfied.

He put off having a bath, no longer a pleasure not while he had to lodge his right leg up on the end to keep the plaster dry. He took his drink out on to the patio, and sat gazing at Venus who was brighter than he'd seen her all Summer bringing to mind one of the anonymous notes.

> *Stars, hide your fires!*
> *Let not light see my black and deep desires*

The night was warm, and he sat too long dwelling on the future. His family came first. Stephie and Kate meant more to him than a job which entailed digging into diseased minds. This present case, like Hampton Court and The Tower sickened him. He was getting tired of being seconded, sent hither and thither to deal with problems facing other forces. He'd resign. Give them six months notice, plenty of time to replace him, then he'd do the things he wanted to do. Teach languages, and do his own research. He'd find Thomas Shaxper, hunt down the Bard's ancestors, much more stimulating and satisfying than digging into the background of corrupt and degenerate twentieth-century characters.

Kate couldn't sleep. She wasn't used to sharing a bed, so she waited patiently for her father to run his bath. He was a long time. She slipped out of bed, crept downstairs and found him in the garden fast asleep.

'Wake up! Wake up, Daddy. You need a bath.'

'That's not all I need, my darling. Not quite all.'

Chapter 7

A solemn air and the best comforter
To an unsettled fancy cure thy brains.

To say the mood in the Royal Shakespeare Theatre
on the following morning was euphoric would be an
understatement. Sally safe and sound. A miracle! The set
builders, the scene painters, the wardrobe staff, the sound
and lighting technicians, the box office, the cleaners,
the actors, the Artistic Director and management were
laughing and crying for joy. All except one. All except
Nigel who could hardly believe the news and when at last
he took it in he could only think of Sally as she was. He
hardly dared think of what she might have become after
living as a recluse with Lorraine for a year.

When Fraser Drummond heard the news he had to
admit to himself that he was pleased and surprised at
the outcome. Finding Sally Siddons unharmed could do
nothing but good for the prestige of the Force. The
media had been summoned to a Press conference in
the circle bar at the Royal Shakespeare for 11 o'clock
that morning, and he fervently hoped Byrd would deal
with it in a more expansive and diplomatic way than he'd
managed at his last encounter. Being pleased with one
aspect of the case didn't mean he'd go along with the
wayward officer from Thames who'd studiously avoided
giving him the low-down on Janet Shaw's murder by
sidestepping questions and asking his own. The Major
wanted everything on computer. Facts. Facts. Facts.
That's what he was going to have. Now the infuriating
man had called on Inspector Hart's services and told him
to get down to Worcester for the second day's racing.
Hart, if rumour was correct, spent too much time on the

turf. A busman's damned holiday, and the police service paying for it!

Viv Mollington was shaken when he learned that his productions had been sabotaged by the woman he most trusted. He was angry with himself for not picking up the signals which he now realised were flaming beacons. How had he been so obtuse? He didn't want to see this execrable woman ever again, didn't trust himself . . . never had he felt such hatred . . . such anger, and strangely, such sorrow. He'd leave the sacking of Lorraine Jefferson to John Butler. How fortunate that Daniel Adkins, her deputy, was an easygoing pragmatic young man who enjoyed a challenge and was quite capable of picking up the pieces. The rehearsal had been at sixes and sevens since the cast had heard the news but now that they were beginning to settle Daniel could carry on with the run-through while he attended the press conference.

For over an hour Stephanie had sat at the breakfast table unable to black out the image, an image of a juggernaut bearing down on her. She couldn't bring herself to clear the table, have a shower, or get dressed. Her legs and arms felt like lead and her body ached in every joint. The pains in her chest were the worst. The seat belt might have saved her from being thrown around, but the constriction left her with a ghastly feeling as if her heart would burst.

Breakfast TV was still on, but she neither saw nor heard it, nor did she hear knocking at the front door.

Laura Fenton didn't waste time, she ran round to the back of the house, peered in at the empty kitchen, found the door locked and being a lithe sixty-three she leapt over the wall surrounding the patio and tugged at the french doors. She could see her daughter in the dining room, sitting like a zombie staring into space.

Stephanie heard her mother's voice, all part of the nightmare she was experiencing, but it took some seconds for the furious banging on the window to get through to her. She rose unsteadily to her feet, and unlocked the door.

'Mum, what are you doing here?'

Her normally undemonstrative mother put her arms round her and kissed her, something she had not done since Stephanie's wedding.

'I've come to stay, so you'll have to get used to the idea.'

'But James might not . . .'

'James invited me and I'm not leaving until you're a thousand per cent better.'

Stephanie heard herself laugh.

'A thousand per cent, Mum, that's what you always used to say.'

The circle bar was full. Byrd had never seen so many attend a press briefing at such short notice. Gerald, Viv, John Butler and Ben stood at the back. For them it was merely another theatrical happening for which they hadn't had to pay. Mayhew and Quinney did a check as reporters from TV, radio, and nationals all crowded in. One smart alick who complained that the bar wasn't open got short shrift from Gerald who told him to quench his thirst in the river restaurant.

Detective Superintendent Byrd had mapped out exactly what he was going to say . . . his parameters were rigid. Nothing about crystals, tarot cards, kidnap or the occult. Nothing either to connect the murder of Janet Shaw with the disappearance of Sally. For the moment all the media gleaned was that Sally had been closeted with Lorraine Jefferson while she came to terms with mental stress and doubts about her acting ability. He made it clear from the outset that there was no question of a sexual relationship.

Viv, at the back of the room, knew the wormers away at truth were there because they wanted high drama and banner headlines. Half-truths didn't satisfy them. They also demanded recent pictures of Sally, pictures of Lorraine, pictures of the chalet. Byrd had anticipated their avid desires and had thwarted them on all counts except one. He'd been in contact with Miss Fairburn at Cedar Road School who'd collected the Browns and driven them to her isolated cottage in the grounds of Castle Ashby, a few miles outside Northampton. Quinney had warned Lorraine not to speak to the Press, but there was no way Byrd could protect the Strachans from the scourge of photographers who descended on them like a plague of locusts, causing mayhem during the last few days of their holiday. They bitterly regretted coming home early, yet had they not done so who would have fed their precious animals?

Every nook and cranny of the chalet was filmed, but a reporter from the local paper knowing the cottage's history waited until his colleagues had melted away before infiltrating, and sitting down with the Strachans in their beamed and inglenooked kitchen.

Nigel was on his own in the Dirty Duck when Byrd and Mayhew came through the door. Perhaps, if he was ever going to tell them, this was the right moment? He'd hated snitchers ever since his school days, but this was something he should get off his chest. He waved rather feebly at the two police officers who lost no time in joining him.

'I'm starving,' said Georgina, 'getting up at 5.30 a.m. and breakfasting before six doesn't suit me. You're not saving these seats for anyone, are you?'

'No. I need to talk to you, something I've been putting off. It didn't feel quite right, but even a small thing . . . ' he hesitated.

'Might be germane to the case? asked Byrd

'Yes, that's what I'm trying to say.'

They listened carefully, forgot all about ordering lunch while Nigel tried to recall everything Janet had said during their last evening together.

It transpired that during lunchtime on the day before she was killed she'd taken sandwiches and a thermos into the Theatre Gardens. She lay on the grass behind some bushes close to one of the wooden benches where Lenny and Alan were sitting. They were having a heated argument which caused the normally lugubrious Alan to curse Lenny, call him a liar and an idiot for the bootless

169

way he'd handled the business. Janet hadn't a clue what they were talking about, but it got really hairy as Lenny tried to convince Alan that the deal was £5,000, not £20,000. He swore the buyer had reneged on his promises because there was already a similar piece of equipment being manufactured by competitors.

The Superintendent sat with his eyes closed. Two more pieces of the jigsaw, but where exactly did they fit? The background was complete, could these irregular shaped pieces be the central pivot?

Nigel stopped short, he liked his audience to watch him, to listen to him, but this strange man was half asleep.

'Don't let me put you off, Nigel,' murmured Byrd, 'Finish the story.'

'There's not much to tell. Alan didn't believe a word, and tore off in a great rage with Lenny chasing after. him.'

Mayhew could sense the change in her boss. He'd entered the pub tired and jaded after a chorus of gibes and unanswerable questions from the Media. Now he was refreshed. Something Nigel had said touched a chord, told him he was on the right track. She too had theories, but first she'd have a go at him. It was about time he shared his thoughts.

'Nigel,' said Byrd grinning, 'if I didn't know you had a rehearsal this afternoon I'd buy you a double whisky.'

The actor relaxed, knew he'd made the right decision.

'I wouldn't say no to a coffee.'

Shortly after lunch Byrd and Mayhew made their way to the Coroner's Court where they had a chance to talk to Mr Wainwright who couldn't enlarge on what he'd told them at the scene of the crime.

There was no reason, the Coroner's officer had said, to defer the inquest. It took less than twenty minutes for the coroner to ascertain the identity of the deceased, when, where, and how the death occurred. The result, a stark and foregone conclusion. *Murder by a person or persons unknown*. Byrd was angry with himself, he felt guilty too, because he should have read the signs, no matter how obscure.

Mayhew unable to stem her tears looked straight ahead making no move to dry her eyes. She felt a comforting hand on hers, a gesture of sympathy, then he placed a handkerchief on her lap solving her predicament. She hadn't told him that shortly before they entered the court Jemmett had passed on two messages. Ben was at 33 waiting to see them, and Keaton had ordered her to be at DHQ by 1800 hours.

Ben who'd followed the gaggle of reporters to the Garrick Inn sat quietly enjoying a beer while listening to the hyperbole bursting from the mouths of the fourth estate and the quieter chat of two Americans who were sitting at the same table.

'Maisie, I'm telling you. An apprentice weaver died here during the plague in 1564.'

'Judie you've gotten it all wrong.'

'No, I haven't. It's the year Shakespeare was born and he was lucky to survive. Then in 1718 this place became an inn, first The Reindeer, then The Greyhound.'

'And then The New Inn,' said Maisie triumphantly.

Ben was fascinated.

'Excuse me, ladies, can you tell me when it became The Garrick?'

Maisie looked at her notes.

'In 1769 after the three-day jubilee initiated by Garrick.'

'Thanks,' he said as he got up to buy another half.

To begin with he'd been fascinated watching reporters who were more outgoing and extravagant than any actors he'd ever met. All with their mobile phones in their hands upstaging each other for the glory of a banner headline, but he soon became bored with their predictable behaviour. He glanced at the rest of the clientele wondering whether they could hear themselves speak. Suddenly he sat up, swallowed hard, and wondered whether his eyes or his memory were deceiving him? There in the corner, unaware he was of interest, sat a man whose face he recognised. He must make contact with Sergeant Mayhew immediately. Ben's brain ticked over like the computers he so expertly manipulated. The only way to reach Georgina was to chat up a reporter, borrow a mobile phone and call the Incident Room. It was easier than he thought, but neither the Superintendent nor the Sergeant were there. Stymied he sat wondering what to do when play was taken out of his court. The man rose, and without a glance in Ben's direction left the pub.

Ben was on his feet, leaving his drink half finished, and praying the stranger wasn't parked in the High Street. It was easy, so easy that Ben waltzed along the street with a broad grin on his face. He followed him down towards the bridge. Half way across they waited for the traffic to clear, before heading towards the Moat House Hotel. Ben followed his quarry into the foyer, saw him collect his key from reception, and take the lift to the third floor. That was all he needed to know, and in a light-hearted mood made his way to 33 Waterside only to find that neither Byrd nor Mayhew had returned.

He kicked his heels in the Incident Room by wandering to and fro between the garden and the kitchen which irritated Jemmett who found it difficult to concentrate.

'Good God!' he yelled, 'look what you've made me do.'

Ben turned to see an irate constable looking at a blank screen.

'I've lost it! I've lost the lot.'

'What did you do?'

'I've no idea.'

'Here let me have a go.'

'You can't do that. This is confidential police business.'

'But there's nothing confidential about a blank screen.'

'No, I suppose there's not, that's the problem. OK, have a go, but be quick. If the Super. walks in I'll be for the high jump.'

'What was the file number?'

'24A.'

Ben tapped away for a few seconds and up came 24A with details of Lenny's background. He stared goggle-eyed. Was the lighting man implicated in Janet's murder?

172

'Don't read it, for God's sake don't read it.'

'No,' said Ben, 'wouldn't dream of it.'

The policeman, breathing a sigh of relief, sat down.

'Thanks,' he said, 'thanks for that. Help yourself to a cold drink.'

'That's what you need,' said Ben.

They'd had a good lunch at the Dirty Duck and Mayhew purposely withheld the messages until they reached the coffee stage. She knew her boss would hare back to the Incident Room to see Ben, giving them both indigestion in the process. Ben was on holiday. He could wait a few minutes.

She was right. As soon as she opened her mouth he was on his feet and back in 33 before his coffee had cooled.

Mayhew thrust the photographs she'd taken in Warwick Castle into Ben's hands.

'Take another look at the man. Make sure, because orientals have a sameness when viewed by occidentals.'

He looked her straight in the eyes, could see himself mirrored there.

'Are you angry with me.'

'No, of course not. I keep thinking about a cup of hot coffee.'

He was puzzled. Shook his head.

'There, that's the man I saw in the Garrick. He's staying at The Moat House, on the third floor, I think.'

'Fantastic! Absolutely fantastic,' she said making an act of attrition.

Fortuitous, thought Byrd, to have the Professor in the right place at the right time, a few chance words in the bar could help the case along. Georgina was curious. 'What would you have done, Ben, if he'd driven off?'

'I thought about that . . . probably taken a taxi and sent The Bill the bill!'

Jemmett sniggered and handed his Super. a sheaf of messages which including the order for Sergeant Mayhew to be at DHQ by 1800 hours.

'What's this all about?' he roared.

'I've no idea, sir.'

He knew. Keaton wanted the low-down on the present case, one way to find out was to send for Mayhew, and what's more he had a legitimate reason. The Chief would present Georgina with a facet of his character the Superintendent had never seen, that of a fatherly figure interested in the well-being of his officers. He'd press home his keenness to promote those in whom he had great trust, and once he'd told her that on 1st July she would attain the rank of Inspector he'd delve into the present case – a friendly chat – find out, by devious means, what was going on.

Byrd had decided to sit down with his sergeant that very afternoon to review the case and share all those insubstantial ideas that were colouring his thinking. They were so near now, near if his intuition hadn't let him down, but his heart to heart could wait until the morning. That way Keaton would be left in the dark, and if he was off beam then his boss wouldn't have the satisfaction of knowing.

At 4.30 p.m. Byrd and Mayhew sat in Gerald's office discussing arrangements for the funeral. Mayhew had already checked with the bank only to be told that Janet's assets amounted to £231, not enough to cover the funeral costs.

'It's no problem,' explained John Butler. 'Equity always makes a grant towards expenses, the company is having a whip-round and if necessary the RSC will make up the difference.'

During the meeting Viv hadn't uttered a word being too discomposed to say what was in his mind, but he had to tackle it.

'We open in four days,' he said quietly, 'during which time we have technicals and dress rehearsals, and an audience to consider. Janet would understand what I'm trying to say. If we could arrange for the service at a time which doesn't conflict . . . doesn't conflict . . .'

Gerald came to the rescue.

'Of course Janet would understand. Why don't we try for 9 a.m. the day after tomorrow?'

'Then,' said Mayhew bitingly, 'a small event like a funeral won't disrupt more important matters.'

'Look at it, how you like,' said Viv sharply, 'this dilemma is something everyone in the profession will understand.'

Gerald again diffused the tension.

'I've talked with the Vicar at Holy Trinity who's agreed to a Memorial Service in a month's time, so I suggest that after the cremation her ashes are scattered under Garrick's tree, in a place she loved, and where she learnt most of her lines.'

Viv and John nodded agreement, and left Gerald to make the arrangements.

Inspector Hart, who was on the crest of a wave following a successful afternoon at the races, drove into the theatre car park as Mayhew drove out. He was dressed in civvies looking every inch the punter, a punter whose wallet was a little thicker than when he left Stratford. Thirty-five pounds thicker, not bad for an afternoon's business which had been spiced with pleasure. Strange thing was he hadn't rated this guy from Thames who was limping around the place dressed in jeans and lurid shirts. Dickybird they called him, well Dickybird had got it right. Guesswork the Super. had laughingly said when he asked him to chat up the bookies, visit the tote and keep an eye on a short man with a curiously flat face who looks like an amiable tortoise. The Super. whose hypothesis was spot on could have been reading the future in a crystal ball.

The young man would have been better off if he'd gone for short odds on the top jockeys. Wouldn't have made a fortune, but he wouldn't have lost it either. Bill Sharkie, an ex-Ladbrooke's man, now running his own business, who had his ear to the ground was most forthcoming, had given him all the dirt. He locked the car and strode across to 33 not noticing the swans, the tourists nor the young man who'd lost his shirt that afternoon on the gee gees.

Georgina was thunderstruck. She'd always known that she was senior officer material, but hadn't expected Detective

Chief Superintendent Keaton to acknowledge the fact. By the 1st of July she'd be Inspector Mayhew. The Chief was unusually forthcoming. He described the cases she'd worked on with a thoroughness that surprised her but, as he took care to point out, her present case with Byrd hadn't yet been documented which could mean more laurels once the truth was told.

It was only when he began delving that she realised, as usual, there were many aspects of the case Dickybird hadn't shared with her. Why had Inspector Hart spent a day at the races? Why spend so much time investigating Lenny's dealings with a Japanese businessman which could have no bearing on the case? Why go on debating the meaning of the quotations when they all knew Lorraine had sent them? And then it struck her . . . the stage manager was always in and out of rehearsals . . . no one could possibly swear she was present in the *Ashcroft Room* between 9.30 and 10 on the morning of Janet's murder. Viv Mollington had been positive that everyone was present. Was that because the rehearsal was running smoothly and he'd imagined Lorraine was in the room? A person on whom he'd built an absolute trust?

Jack Keaton was distinctly uptight. What was the matter with the woman? She'd hardly told him a thing, in fact most of his questions had been batted back in a subtle female way. She was clever this one, no doubt about it, but she was covering up for the insufferable James Byrd. He'd been going to offer her a drink, but he bade her a terse 'goodnight', and that was that.

As she left DHQ she picked up a copy of the *Police Review* and sat in the car scanning the appointments column. There were two jobs in Edinburgh, one which meant going back into uniform, and the other in CID. She'd think about it for a day or two . . . didn't fancy uniform . . . she liked bright vibrant colours and calf length skirts.

Still sitting in the car she thought about the questions Keaton had flung at her, questions she couldn't answer. Oh yes, she had theories, but they needed to be shared. She was angry with James Byrd. Any investigation called

176

for a two-way dialogue. As she hammered the digits on the mobile phone she thought up a hundred excuses why she should give up the case. Byrd, who was talking to Inspector Hart when the phone rang, was in an unusually equable mood.

'Congratulations Georgina on your preferment.' were the words he uttered before she had a chance to vent her spleen.

'You knew!'

'Not officially. Heard it on the grapevine.'

'We need to talk, get things in the open,' she said tersely.

He half smiled to himself as he heard the aggro in her voice.

'Yes, Inspector we do. I had thought about running through the case in the morning, but that may be too late. You'd better get back here pronto, we've a night's work ahead of us.'

'Yes sir,' she said softly.

Inspector Hart left knowing he'd champion Byrd against any of his critics. He'd chance his arm and do what the Super. had asked. The man had vision and a miraculous way with fractious bank managers. It had taken no more than ten minutes to find out from John Butler that a certain theatre technician had his salary paid directly into a Stratford bank which was managed by a Mr Kenton who, in turn, obliquely described the state of his client's account.

PC Jemmett, although quite excited at the turn of events, was annoyed with himself for not solving the murder when he had all the details on the computer. He was totally at sea, not realising it was all down to the methods used by the officer-in-charge.

Laura answered the phone, Laura who'd given up her daily round of golf and evening game of bridge to care for her daughter. She was enjoying herself. It was the first time her son-in-law had ever asked a favour. The first time he'd made her feel needed.

'Laura, is everything OK?'

'Yes.'

'How's Stephie?'

She hated the shortening of her daughter's name, but after an infinitesimal pause she answered him.

'Stephanie's fine. She's sitting in the garden playing Monopoly with Kate. Shall I fetch her?

'No. Don't disturb her. Tell her I'm sorry but I won't be home tonight, but with luck I'll take a couple of days off next week.'

'She's OK, James. Don't worry.'

'Thanks, Laura, you're a great support.'

As she replaced the phone her eyes misted over, but she kept the tears at bay. A great support, he'd said.

'Sir, sir . . .'

'Yes, Jemmett?'

'I'd like to stay on when my relief comes on duty, sir, in case you need me.'

The hardened policeman looked at the eager young face of a lad whose antenna, he was pleased to note, was definitely working. A lad who sensed a breakthrough so why deprive him of the excitement?

'A good idea, Constable, but your next job is of prime importance. Get out there and buy sandwiches for six. No one thinks straight on an empty stomach.'

'Yes, sir.'

'Oh, and bring some cake. I've got a sweet tooth.'

Jemmett grinned. Sometimes the Super. was quite human. He was out shopping, as Byrd thought he would be, when Georgina arrived in a fighting mood.

'Isn't it about time, sir, that you levelled?'

'Keaton's curious is he? You told him very little, of course.'

'There was hardly anything he didn't already know, though I couldn't tell him, could I, that we haven't really checked up on Lorraine Jefferson? Where was she, this will-o'-the-wisp, between 9.30 and 10 on the morning of the murder?'

'You think she knifed Janet?'

'It's possible. A few minutes out of rehearsal where no one would miss her because they were totally wrapped up in the drama. Their concentration amazes me. The deed done she would have returned to the wrong play.'

'What do you mean?'

'They should have been doing *Macbeth*!

'What about the knife and the bloody clothes?'

'She could have worn a hip length anorak and stuffed it into that capacious bag she carries, along with the knife'.

'It's a reasonable premise, Georgina, but she's not a killer, despite the fact that the quotes indicated she was thinking about it. She was afraid of herself, of what she might do. She'd grown fond of Sally, but if she'd let her go it would have been "goodbye" for ever to another job in the theatre.'

'All right, sir, so that's one theory demolished so hadn't you better tell me what's in your devious mind?'

'Quinney's in the theatre right now waiting for Lenny to arrive. He'll bring him over for a lengthy grilling.'

'But what about tonight's show?'

'The lighting's computerised, so there's no problem, If they haven't a spare operator Ben can do it. He's assured me he still belongs to the union.'

'You think Lenny murdered Janet?'

'Let's keep an open mind until we've talked to him.'

She sat silently thinking about aspects of the case which hadn't so far been explained and then another extraordinary idea hit her. Not possible . . . too far out . . . not for a handful of silver . . .

Jemmett breezed in with his bag of Marks and Spencer goodies including a bottle of Piesporter.

'Thought you needed a tonic, sir.'

'I'll say this for you, Constable, you have style, but the bottle can wait. Just shove the kettle on.'

While the eager PC sorted out crockery and spread out an array of cakes. Mayhew, who needed air, sat on the patio admiring the kerria japonica while she rethought her latest hypothesis.

Her boss browsed through the *Police Review* she'd left on the window seat, and was disturbed to find ticks against two appointments in Edinburgh. She couldn't go . . . she mustn't go . . . it wouldn't be the same . . . no one could fill her place. Only then did he realise he'd become too fond. Kaleidoscopic scenes flashed through his mind . . . their aggro and unspoken reconciliation during the Tower case . . . a brief look, no more, which said a thousand words . . . the expression on her face when she thought he'd been injured at Hampton Court . . . his joy when Sir Charles released her to play the role of a management consultant . . . Stephie's irritability one evening when, without warning, Georgina arrived at the house. How obtuse he'd been, but why Edinburgh? Was she going home, or was she making a timely escape, which might be better for them both before a small seed blossomed?

Lawrence found Mr Kuprati alone in the bar, and without a by your leave sat down at the same table. They were soon chatting away as if they'd been buddies for years. Mr Kuprati was lonely, his was a lonely business, and this tall, broad shouldered American from Princeton was a breath of fresh air.

At no time did the word Cambridge pass Lawrence's lips. He was an American on holiday with tickets for two productions and a tour of the theatre on his final day. Mr Kuprati, skilfully avoiding mentioning the theatre, talked about his family, his home, and his hobbies, most notably golf. It took some careful probing to discover the nature of his job. Not theatre as Lawrence had expected, but cameras, cheap cameras, which had made a fortune for his garrulous companion. Now, and this was the rub, Kuprati wanted to diversify, do something, say, in computers that no one had ever tackled. For computers, thought Lawrence, substitute lighting, but he was in a new field, still learning. Might be too much of a gamble but *koketsu ni irazunba koji wo ezu* said Kuprati which the Professor read as nothing ventured, nothing gained.

When Lawrence made a move to go the Japanese stood up and bowed before telling him that this had been his first long exchange with a stranger. The English, he'd said, were reserved, it took an American to make contact so effortlessly.

180

The Professor took the lift to the third floor and from his room telephoned James Byrd.

'Tomorrow,' he said, 'subject leaves for his home base. Seems undecided about the deal, may have called it off.'

Ironic, thought Byrd as he replaced the phone. If there'd been no deal, there would have been no murder.

Quinney arrived with an angry and worried Lenny in tow.

'What the dickens are you lot up to?'

'Sit down, and take it easy,' said Mayhew.

'I've a show to run. Ben's a bloody rookie, you can't expect him to cope?'

'He'll cope,' smiled Byrd to himself, 'he's a wizard with computers. Jemmett can vouch for that.'

The constable looked at him flabbergasted. How did the Super. know Ben had retrieved a lost file?

'Get on with it,' yelled Lenny.

'Let me tell you what we know.'

Not what we know, thought Mayhew, what my boss has guessed, and he's now trying it out for size.

'Mr Kuprati returns to Japan tomorrow.'

'My God!' The lighting wizard looked at them ashen faced. He rounded on Quinney. 'You said I was to be questioned about the murder. The business with Kuprati is private, it's got nothing to do with Janet's murder.'

'It may have everything to do with it, Mr Richards,' said Byrd turning to Jemmett who was finding the drama more exciting than any TV drama he'd ever watched. 'Pour me another cup of tea, Constable.'

Quinney sitting on the stairs surveying the scene thought it the oddest interview room he'd ever encountered. His Super. sitting on the window-seat with his plastered leg on the occasional table looked comfortably set for the night.

The only sound was Jemmett pouring the tea. Quinney recognised the ploy. Make the interviewee uncomfortable, make him feel guilty, make him feel he's going to be here all night.

'No hurry,' the Super. was saying, 'I have all the time in the world.'

'Well what do you want to know?' asked Lenny Richards, his South London accent now more pronounced.

'Take your time, but you'll not leave here until you've told us everything about your deal with Kuprati.'

Lenny didn't take his time. There was no point. They knew too much.

'The Jap was the wrong damn man. Didn't understand lighting, I'd have done better talking to an English firm.'

'So what was the deal?'

'£50,000 was his first offer, that's when he knew the equipment would be on trial for two years. Then we heard other manufacturers were also experimenting with new boards, nothing new you see, except the black light. That's not its final name, it's what we call it while we're experimenting.'

'Have you actually tried it out? asked Mayhew.

'No.'

'Why not?'

'Viv would have gone bananas, used it in every show, and then everyone in the business would've heard about it.

'So didn't the inventor complain when it wasn't used?'

'I made adjustments to make sure it never functioned properly when Michael Gibbs was in the theatre. He kept going back to the drawing board which gave me more time.'

At that moment Inspector Hart arrived.

'Good God! Not another bleeding copper.'

Inspector Hart nodded to Byrd, gave him the thumbs up and joined Quinney on the stairs.

'Five of you bastards here wasting time on a deal that didn't come off when you should be hunting for Janet's murderer.'

'You, Mr Richards,' said Byrd with loathing, 'were instrumental in her murder, but for you she would still be alive.'

Mayhew closed her eyes. At last she'd drawn the threads together and could understand why her boss had been so chary of making a final judgement.

'Don't talk such crap.'

'I believe, Kuprati's first offer amounted to £50,000, but was finally reduced to £5,000 for services rendered. In other words there will be no Japanese input into the latest lighting technology.'

Lenny was speechless. He glanced at Mayhew whose face was like stone, then back to Byrd.

'How the hell,' he gasped, 'did you find out?'

'We didn't, but a dead actress did.'

'She couldn't have.

'Tell me, Mr Richards, who else was affected by the reduction?'

'No one.'

'Who knew all about your nasty little stratagems? Who was blackmailing you?'

'No comment.'

'Two and a half thousand, the blackmailer's share of your ill-gotten gains, wasn't enough. Was it?'

Lenny jumped to his feet.

'How the hell did you find out?'

'Conducting business on a bench in the Theatre Gardens was a little thoughtless wasn't it, especially at lunchtime in a place where actors sun themselves and devour sandwiches?

'You mean . . . oh my God . . . you mean Janet heard . . . and . . .' The Superintendent nodded. Every vestige of colour left Lenny's face leaving him looking like an old man. 'Janet,' he whispered, 'I never meant . . . truly I never . . .'

Byrd looked at Inspector Hart for confirmation.

'Yes. The knife, a bloody shirt and trousers were stuffed in a bag under Alan Hunt's bed. Didn't have to break in, used my Access card which seemed right and proper.'

'You effected an entry, Inspector,' said Byrd with a wry grin, 'and that's all that matters. Now let us go and arrest the little runt.'

'You can't,' yelled Lenny. 'you'll put the mockers on the show. The sound's essential.'

Jemmett, open mouthed, wondered how the Super. would take that.

'Of course. How many ways into the sound box?'
'Only one, from the circle.'
'OK. Let's get up there and wait. Mr Richards you'd better get back, and keep your mouth shut.'
'No, no I can't,' whispered the shaken man. 'I can't do it . . . all I can think about is Janet . . . let Ben carry on.'
'Very well.'

Alan slipped out of his box during the interval to buy an ice cool orangeade from the circle bar. He was eaten up with anger at the thought of the dirty trick Lenny had pulled. He couldn't swallow one word of such an unlikely tale. Why would the Jap suddenly withdraw? No one in his right senses would opt out of a £50,000 deal which in the end could net him millions. Of course the deal was going ahead otherwise why hand over £5,000? He'd deal with Lenny, scare the shit out of him, give him twenty-four hours in which to hand over the money otherwise John Butler would learn what was going on. After all he'd nothing to lose. Both bank managers, unknown to each other, were pressing him to settle his overdrafts. Eight and a half grand he owed Lloyds, and Yorkshire were chasing him for seven. Funny thing how both those arrogant bastards, barricaded behind their vast highly polished desks, uniformly dressed in dark blue suits and quiet ties believed he'd been offered his flat at a ridiculously knock-down price because the landlord couldn't get him out.

He'd been unlucky recently, but that would change. Worcester hadn't helped. That little rat of a jockey had sworn blind the race was fixed. Agamemnon would win, he'd said, straight up, he'd said. The damn thing hadn't even made the first three, so that was another grand down the chute. Lenny would hand over twenty-five grand tomorrow or that was the end of his career. He owed him. They'd have been in shtuck if Janet had talked. At least he'd been in time, there'd not been a whisper. Ben's arrival had shaken him, but that was all related to Sally's disappearance.

Tomorrow he'd get rid of the evidence. Drive to his

sister's place outside Tewkesbury, burn the shirt in her garden incinerator and chuck the knife in the river. He wondered, humming softly to himself, why the murder enquiry was so low-key? Nothing to go on, that's what. He'd never rated that policeman who limped around in a gaudy shirt, not from the first moment he'd poked his head in the sound box, nor the woman who was so easy on the eye. Pity he hadn't finished him off on his first day. Lorraine, who'd thought it a joke, was shattered when she learned he'd taken the trap right down, and Lenny nearly had an apoplectic fit, but neither had dared mention it.

As he carried the orangeade back to his box he saw a familiar face, someone he felt he should know, but the guy ignored him. Suddenly, a spur of the moment decision, he decided to have it out with Lenny. Hastily he gulped down the drink, plonked the glass on a table, eased his way through the crowd and entered the lighting box. All four police officers hidden among the crowd realised what was happening. He'd find Ben in charge, cotton on and make a dash for it. Quinney was nearest, he stood blocking the exit waiting for Alan Hunt to emerge. It was Mayhew who saved the day. She caught a glimpse of Ben making his way to the Gents' loo and grabbed him.

'Don't return to the box until you hear the bar bell.'

'Why?'

'Alan's in there. If we have to take him now it will ruin the show.'

He leant back against the wall, it took some seconds for him to take it in.

'You mean he's the . . . the . . .' She nodded.

'Alan murdered Janet? he whispered. She nodded again.

'Pull yourself together, Ben, you've got to get through the second half.'

She left him standing there and found Byrd seated near the bar well out of Alan's sightline when he emerged from the lighting box.

In the meantime Alan stood fuming as he watched the audience returning. Just like Lenny to take his time. A red cue light flickered on as the bar bell echoed in the small

185

corridor. No time now, an imminent sound effect was needed as the houselights were dimmed. He wrenched open the door and ran. Funny! The guy he felt he knew was standing by the window showing no sign of returning to his seat, but he gave it no more thought as he flicked up a switch and the sound of waves breaking upon the shore filled the theatre.

It was when Ariel was singing 'Merrily, merrily shall I live now' that he placed the man. In the back of his mind there was a vague picture of him queueing at the tote, almost certainly the same guy whose back was to him in the bar crush. The man Bill Sharkie was chatting up, the man who drove into the theatre car park shortly after 6 o'clock. The bastard had followed him.

They were on to him and there was no way out. They'd have all the exits covered. No way down, but they wouldn't expect him to go up. He slipped out into the darkened auditorium, moved silently behind the back row and crept out through a side exit. The usher, who didn't recognise him in the dark, was enjoying the play. She always liked this bit with its tuneful music, but she liked it most of all because she knew her stint was almost at an end. She could get back to the telly and watch the boxing, something far more dramatic, because she'd no idea how it would end.

Alan made his way up to the balcony testing all the cupboard doors along the corridor, but they were firmly locked leaving him only one alternative. He peered into the bar. Damn! Olga was still tidying up. His objective had been to hide behind the counter, but the ramparts would do, that's what Lenny always called the outer area. He'd climb over the parapet and lie hidden on the narrow ledge at the near end where he'd not be visible. That would do. They'd not come up, they'd go down. Keep an eye on his car. Watch his flat. Damn, he hadn't thought it out. Hadn't made contingency plans. Couldn't go to his sister's, she'd never wear it, but his Gran would keep her mouth buttoned. Her blue eyed boy would never kill a defenceless girl.

He waited until Olga eased the bottles out of the optics

and while her back was to him he slipped through the sliding glass door on to the terrace, and clambered over the parapet. It was his lucky day. The thin strip of lead roof on which he lay was bone dry. If she peered out before closing the doors she'd not see him.

Prospero reached the epilogue and waited for the island's magical sounds to reverberate round the theatre. No magic. Only silence. Damn! Alan was late with the cue, but Josh was too experienced an actor to let the lack of sound throw him. He threw his cloak on the shore and crossed downstage towards the audience into a badly lit area. He glanced up at the control room as if praying to celestial gods.

Ben who'd seen the play the night before got the message, knew there'd been a hitch. Slowly throughout the last twenty lines he brought up a downstage spot which reached its zenith as Josh, looking for all the world like the new Messiah, said 'Let your indulgence set me free.'

It's not what Viv intended but it worked. The audience was on its feet clapping and cheering, but Viv who'd slipped into the director's box shuddered at the melodramatic finale and vowed it would never ever happen again.

Ben, who'd imagined the lack of sound was due to the fact that the Alan had been arrested, dutifully brought up the houselights and killed everything else. He felt good, much more satisfying than sitting in an office dreaming up insurance programmes. He waited for the audience to leave and watched as the ushers checked to make sure no one had left jackets or bags behind before he extinguished the houselights.

As he left the box Byrd pounced on him.

'Is he still there?'

'No.'

'What do you mean?'

'He can't be. He missed the final cue.'

'Damnation!' He said a lot more than that under his breath. Ben listened as the policeman spoke over the blower to Quinney, Hart and Mayhew.

187

'He's done a bunk.'

'Not this way' said Hart. 'Not on your nelly.'

'Nor this way,' said Quinney.

Then thought Byrd, Mayhew must have him in her sights. Her disembodied voice whispered in his ear. 'I caught a glimpse of him going up, he must be in the gods.'

'Ben get back in there and switch on the houselights.'

'OK.'

'Georgina, which side are you?'

'Audience left.'

'Right. I'll come up the other stairs.'

Quinney and Hart heard the interchange.

'I'm on my way, sir.'

'Me too,' said Hart.

They examined every row, but there was no way he could have hidden under the seats; they were all in the upright position, had to be, according to Licensing Regulations.

At that moment Gerald Maitland came rushing in.

'What's up? What have you lost?'

'Not what,' said Byrd, 'it's whom.'

'We want Alan Hunt,' said Mayhew.

'So does Viv. He wants to see him right now. He's hopping mad.'

'Well Viv will have to wait at least twenty years,' said Byrd sardonically, 'because we're going to nail the bastard first.'

Gerald was shaken.

'You think Alan murdered Janet?'

'I don't think, I know.' Then an idea flashed through his mind. 'We'll take a look in the balcony bar.'

'He'll not be there,' said Gerald, 'There's nowhere to hide.'

'Not for us six footers, but you'd be surprised how a short, slightly built man can make use of the smallest spaces. There must be cupboards or . . .' he didn't finish. 'Come on Gerald, I hope you've got your keys with you.'

The four police officers converged on the bar and

waited while Gerald unlocked the sliding glass door to the terrace. Quinney was first through followed by Mayhew and Byrd. They automatically moved to the centre while Inspector Hart, who thought it a wild goose chase, stayed put in the bar. No man in his right mind would come up here. Perhaps the Super. was as mad as rumour would have it?

Mayhew didn't stop to look at the view, she walked to the far end carefully examining the flat roof and the trunking for the heating system. She bent double over the parapet and looked to her left. She couldn't believe her eyes. There were two small shoes standing on end which moved as she stared at them, and then a glimpse of dark blue jeans, but she was unable to see the rest of the figure. She shouted at Byrd.

'Look over the wall at the far end, sir.

He didn't need to. He knew.

'OK Hunt,' he yelled, 'stand up, you've nowhere to go.'

Alan shivered. This was the end. The rest of his life would be spent in prison. Nothing could be more horrific. He'd heard of the gruesome treatment meted out to child molesters, and sexual perverts, but what would happen to a murderer who'd killed a defenceless girl? He'd been beaten up at school, never able to stand up for himself, the smallest in the pack and fair game. Quinney made a move.

'If you come anywhere near me I'll shoot you,' screamed Alan.

That stopped Quinney in his tracks who saw neither his quarry nor a gun.

'Hunt,' roared Byrd, 'the penalty for killing a policeman will be life with no remission, so think about it.'

Alan, who hadn't a gun, knew what he had to do. They saw his petrified expression as he gingerly got to his feet. Byrd waited no longer, he limped towards him and as he did so realised too late what was about to happen. He rushed at the frightened man, forgetting the pain in his leg, forgetting everything except the desire to save life. He lunged forward trying to catch hold of Hunt's arm but only

189

succeeded in grabbing the tail of his shirt. An unearthly scream reverberated against the wall of the theatre as the body of the soundman hurtled downwards.

'Good God!' said Gerald in horror. 'He's done a Quasimodo.'

In silence they peered over the balcony at the inert figure spreadeagled on the pavement eighty feet below.

'Poor bugger,' said Hart who'd no head for heights, and couldn't bear to look down, 'what a way to go. He gambled once too often.'

James Byrd felt sick. It need never have happened. The killer should have been *taken at the flood*. Taken the moment he realised that Alan Hunt, the middle-aged technician with the gentle face of a tortoise, was the murderer.

Epilogue

Neither Sir Charles nor Fraser Drummond were pleased with the outcome. The Chief Constable of Warwickshire had wanted the publicity of a court case. He wanted the public to hear day after day for weeks on end how the police, with incredible speed, had apprehended the killer, but Sir Charles had a different problem.

This was the third time Byrd had played his fish with too long a line. First The Tower, then Hampton Court, and now this. Had he arrested Hunt before the performance this tragic-opera finale would never have occurred. *The play's the thing*, he thought irritably, which had coloured the whole operation. Byrd had to do everything in his own inimitable way, never by the book.

Detective Superintendent Byrd who saw his Chief Constable on the following day was ordered to take two weeks sick leave. Time in which to repair the aggravated damage to his injured foot caused by racing around without the aid of either crutches or sticks.

Sir Charles smiled wryly to himself as James Byrd left the office. A maverick with imagination. One of his best officers whom he desperately wanted to use on the Bodleian Case, but he couldn't afford any slip-ups. Too many big guns involved. The Home Secretary had categorically stated that the whole business must be kept under wraps. Byrd was the man, Byrd had the scholarship, Byrd had the intuition, but could he ever hope to change him?